THE UNINVITED

A Southern Ghost Story

JEREMY BILLINGSLEY

PublishAmerica
Baltimore

First printing

ISBN: 1-4137-4688-8
PUBLISHED BY PUBLISHAMERICA, LLLP
www.publishamerica.com
Baltimore

Printed in the United States of America

THE GHOST HUNTER

ONE

The Meeting

Alec Bradshaw sat on the couch amid a plume of dust that made him cough, pushed away invisible webs that tickled his neck; he glanced about the filthy room before settling his eyes on the woman who claimed the entire house had just been cleaned.

God she's fine, he thought, noticing her disheveled black hair, a countenance of one who had just awakened and still wore what must be her bedtime clothes—a thin tee and a pair of gray shorts. And on the heels of his extemporaneous thought: *What a place for a haunting*.

He sat his coffee down and smiled at the black woman in the recliner across from him. Her legs crossed, a bare foot dangling. Looking around again, he noticed the room: elegant, if not for the dust and dirt. The only audible sounds were a ticking clock and the gentle hum of the air conditioner. It was her turn to speak, he decided. She had, after all, set the appointment for this hour of the morning, and had obviously forgotten, here at her home that she had been so adamant about giving exact directions. He decided as the clock chimed the half-hour, this supposition wasn't fair; her predicament lent more importance than a meeting with some amateur problem-solver that may or may not be of any use.

He answered her questions as she spoke slowly. She seemed distracted, her words were heavy, so and it gave him chance enough to look around the one room he had so far seen, as well as reflect on the house's general appearance. From the outside it was two-story, possibly a third with attic space; it was an older home and he knew she had inherited and lived in it most of her life. The living room was tasteful, the décor lenitive, the lighting subtle. He guessed she hadn't changed things much since she took over. She smiled—lips pursed—drawing his attention away from the residence back to her, then asked the question he had most come to expect.

"Are you psychic?"

He emphatically shook his head, even chuckled a little. She asked if he had any special equipment and he showed her a digital camera that could take stills or video, a micro-cassette tape recorder, and his laptop. She asked about his credentials—a degree in parapsychology or something—and he shook his head again. English major, he told her, he had originally planned to teach while working on the *Great American Novel*. She asked what happened. He saddened when he answered.

"Life."

There was silence broken only by the slurping of hot coffee. She offered to refill his cup, complete with milk and sugar, and he accepted, chastising himself for checking out her body as she walked to and from the kitchen. She bent at the waist when she handed him his cup, her t-shirt dangling just enough. He opened the laptop and pulled up what he had of her file.

"What do you do, exactly?"

He glanced over the report. "They come back for a reason. Either that or I think they come back to watch over us." There was this family in Ohio, third-generation Irish, lived on the same homestead as their ancestors who first got off the boat. They were seeing a lot of things; things being moved and glances of people walking or watching them. Most were dressed in older style clothes, but one or two they recognized as the husband's parents. They were watching out for the kids, watching over the farm that had been in their name for nearly a century.

He typed something then folded the notebook down. "They started appearing when he and his wife were having financial troubles, and he was thinking about selling."

She sipped her coffee. "Did you see anything?"

He shook his head.

"Have you ever seen anything?"

Alec felt his lips tighten as he recalled memories not easily repressed. He opened the notebook back up, quickly changing the subject back to her. He reviewed the file aloud, for her benefit: Aisha Jones, 28—*my age*, he thought, and wondered where that came from—African-American, a single schoolteacher, only child, no offspring. Things are breaking throughout the house, lights are flickering, footsteps on stairs, mostly at night. And then there was the dirt problem.

Glass shattered.

He looked up and their eyes locked. Together they stood and walked into the kitchen. They stared at the black puddle on the floor, littered with bits and chunks of the glass carafe. He reached with his free hand and unplugged the coffeemaker.

"So," she said with a huff, "you're pretty tan for a guy that hunts ghosts."

He nodded, said he didn't want to be some pasty scholar. But his eyes were fake, really hazel; the contacts were blue. "Pot was probably old. They can only last so long, and they just crack."

"You work out?"

He nodded again. After a brief hesitation, they knelt and began to clean the mess together. Afterward they returned to the living room, only this time she sat next to him on the sofa, thigh to thigh, holding his hand.

"I help them complete their mission."

It had been awhile since Alec Bradshaw had known any type of companionship outside of working. Betrayed as he felt, it had taken time to come to grips, and now he felt himself start to open up to a woman so similar in countenance—different, physically, she didn't have green eyes or shoulder length brown hair. It wasn't a flood of emotion, just a simple squeeze of his hand, a grain of empathy and all his heart could spare.

"Do you know who the spirit is?"

"My mother."

Aisha spoke of her mother and her last days with love; her father she mentioned with a cold tongue. He was stern to the point of abusive; whether that had any bearing on her being an only child, or vice versa, she wasn't sure, but where her father lacked a heart her mother more than made up for. Alzheimer's, therefore, was a blessing, when Aisha's mother was diagnosed. It was God's way of repressing the hardships of His servant's life.

She swallowed hard, gripped his hand tighter. They didn't move as she spoke. The sternness of her father exceeded his life, followed his wife to her grave in that she could not deviate from his last will and testament in the slightest.

"She couldn't even if she wanted to, toward the end," Aisha corrected.

Alec took all this in quietly, feeling more empathic than he could ever remember. He listened as she spoke of her childhood, of a father who wanted his only child to follow in his footsteps, and of the disappointment that led to a distempered home when she chose education as her field of study.

"What did he do?" Alec asked.

"Law," she answered and named off a few of the larger cases her father had tried. Alec didn't recognize any of them.

His own mind began to wander, and he gave the excuse that he had to clear his head to get ready for tonight. He advised her to get out of the house—if she had a friend go there and rest—get some things done around town. He would try to not make much noise tonight. She said it didn't matter, she wouldn't sleep anyway. He stressed again finding a restful place to go, if she planned to be up, and promised he'd be back at dusk.

She didn't let go of his hand as he reached the door. Instead her eyes gave a plea. "Stuff happens in the daytime, too."

He gave her a reassuring smile, and lent another grain of empathy. His fingers caressed her smooth jaw line. Inwardly he wouldn't confront his present actions. Much to his surprise, and surely hers as well, they hugged before he walked out the door.

He didn't know Chicago well, but he found a park near the lake with a paved trail where joggers lapped him as he strolled with hands in pockets, finally allowing himself the questions. Was he attracted to her? Yes. Physically, and then there was that familiarity, that sense that he knew her because her character was such a facsimile. His thoughts had drifted back to the beginning over recent months, but as he walked along they were ordered, keeping rhythmic time with the lapping of the waves driven by the cool spring breeze. There were so many deaths that led him here, and each step brought each past face to mind. He spent hours walking slowly, reminiscing, letting the ghosts massage his faculties, release the tension of repression and revive his origins. Regret left his face turned down, his eyes locked with the ground, unable to see the beautiful sky warming above him. He realized it wasn't always good to remember.

Just over a year ago his brother and sister-in-law had been in an accident. For six months he paid no attention to the little girl left behind, his own son, his own wife. For six months he abandoned them, lost in grief, and then Lisa did something he never expected from her.

The man called once, after the tryst, and Alec had answered.

This last half-year on the road made little sense to him. He wasn't sure why this occupation fell into him, but it was profitable. He had seen a lot, written nearly all of it down in a notebook, and hoped to some day write it. He kept enough money for himself to eat now and then, to travel, to sleep in a hotel when he wasn't staying at a house or building—and most recently, his clients had begun reimbursing his travel expenses and room and board—and the rest went to penitence. He had made a couple of trips home to see his son, his niece. Lisa he saw also, and while she didn't seem to care to see him, he found himself missing her. Rationality told him why she had done what she did, that she was telling the truth about it being a one-time thing. Rationality also had a small voice in matters of the heart.

He walked, cold all over, as the afternoon rolled into dusk; the darkening sky reminded him that he had an obligation to fill. There was a client who needed help with her ghosts. He looked up to the indigo clouds, his face emotionless, only his eyes to show the sadness, and wondered if he'd ever gather strength enough to rest his own ghosts.

When he returned to Aisha's house, she asked if he was ready and he said yes, then asked her.

"Sometimes they don't like help," he warned as he checked the battery in his camera and his tape recorder. They walked to her second floor; most of the activity had been centered there, recently. Two mirrors faced each other, stretching nearly the length of the hall. He had to push away a conjured memory. He sat near the stairs, turned his camera on and sat it beside him. She took a nearby seat, her back against the wall, and as the sun set outside she asked if they should turn on some lights.

"No."

They waited.

They could hear the clock tick downstairs, like a metronome for their own symphony about to begin. She whispered if it was all right to talk, and he said he didn't see why not, his tone almost regular. When she spoke again she took a similar tone, a slight whisper that made her voice husky.

Something told him it would start with the stairs; his eyes were focused on that point.

"Any family of your own?"

He thought of his brother. Cory had immediately fallen in love with the roommate. Lisa O'Connell was the one Alec had fallen for. Then he spoke aloud.

"*Hacimos ruidos por la noche.*"

stairs in the dark. When the voice started it was far off, like her mother was calling her down for dinner. Aisha was called by name, and two more steps were taken.

He stood, coaxed her to her feet, told her to call back to her mother. She was shivering and sweating and her voice cracked as she raised it.

"I'm here, mother."

Everything fell silent.

They looked at each other. Pipes groaned, the house settled. Alec reached for her hand, found it, felt her grip tighten. They waited. A cool wind picked up and the door next to them opened slowly. They caught a glimpse of the bedroom inside, pastels with oak trim and furniture.

The door slammed shut.

Things began smashing, a noise like a scream echoed through the halls and rooms, and the door began vibrating. From inside they could hear drawers being ripped from the dresser, glass shattering. There was a loud thump. Aisha looked at him, told him it was her mother's old room, and the wind nearly knocked them over. Alec braced himself against the rail, grabbed Aisha. He felt the wood splinter and looked behind, down to the hardwood floor. She tore from his grasp then, and he couldn't hold on to her. She raced to the door, screaming for her mother. Alec tried to stop her but she forced the door open. Then she froze.

Standing to her side, he couldn't see directly into the room. But he saw her jump, then hold out her hands. She called, "Mother" several times, slowly, even stepped toward the door. Then she stopped. She took a step back and a scream erupted from her lungs. The door shut on her. Alec caught her from behind as she slumped into him, sank down, her head resting against his chest. He knelt and laid her back, cradling her head in his arms.

Everything was silent again; he didn't realize it till he saw her eyes close. He stroked her cheek. One hand moved to her chest; he could feel her heart thumping. He put a finger to her lips, parted them, felt shallow breath. Gently working his arms underneath, he carried her into her bedroom, laid her on the bed. He removed her sandals and covered her up, then touched her cheek again, knelt and kissed her forehead.

Downstairs he sat, sipping on coffee from a new carafe, listening to the house settle and nothing else. He really had nothing to think about in this case, except where to find what the ghost was looking for. As dawn came he realized that neither he nor Aisha were going to get rest today; they were going to turn the house upside down.

His hand trembled from the amount of caffeine he had ingested, and his mind switched to the ghost story he told her earlier tonight. His grandfather had entertained them as little children with the tale—once, as they sat around the hearth, the decorated tree in the corner the only light, naked of presents that would soon complete it—and his mother and grandmother chastised the old man for telling such a story to an eight- and six-year-old. His grandfather had given a hoot then, slapped his knee, said it was just a story. Neither Alec nor Cory got much sleep that night.

The morning started off very differently for Lisa. She stood in the kitchen, stared at the dawn through the window as she sipped her coffee. The sounds from last night were fading, sporadic sounds resounding from a shell of memories that won't be forgotten. They used to frighten her; now she found herself sad.

He had left them there—for her it boiled down to that. Soon her son would wake, and not long after that her girl would too. It would be up to Lisa to dress and feed them, to drive them to school, to wait—it was summer vacation for her, now, so all she had throughout the day was to wait in this house—and then to pick them up, feed them again, undress them, bathe them and put them to bed. Then she would wait again, listening to the night stir up the sounds, wait for her son to have a nightmare or her niece to dream/see her parents, and wait a little longer till the sun rose. This had been her day yesterday, and it would be her day again tomorrow. It had been her life for six months now, and for the millionth time she asked herself if it was enough, if she was happy.

It was wearing on her, to be perfectly honest. She could, standing in the blue rays streaming through the window, afford to be honest. She was happy she had the children, and a part of her that felt petty and selfish was happy that all the children had was her. But even with the disenchanted spirits that spoke nightly, providing extraordinary voices for an otherwise normal home, she had fallen into a chasm of necessity, where the walls were too steep to climb and all the canyon could show her was what she needed to survive. Nothing new, and other than the children nothing really hers: the house belonged to his grandparents, then his parents, as did all its belongings and all its memories. By whatever rights of ownership she supposed that meant all this was his now. But Alec wasn't here, and she felt more responsible—she felt more liable—for this life than just some caretaker who took to their duties complacently when the true owner was away. The day would come when the prodigal son would return, and Alec would probably want to claim what he thinks is his, and that day a stairwell would appear to lead her out of the chasm. Would she fight him; she would not concede. They had worked together once and there was something undeniable, buried underneath all her anger for him. It was the one thing she wasn't sure she could afford to be honest about, especially in this morning light in a house his grandparents built, before the children woke.

She missed him. There was more, but she could not say it yet, so she sipped her coffee and pushed all those thoughts out of her head, coolly replacing them with an ordered list of what she would have to do this morning, to get from point A to point B. Never mind she had more than memorized that list—she had committed her life to it. It became all she thought about, until the children woke, and the night sounds ceased while the sun was up. She would take them to school, then come home, and wait, watching the sun play with the shadows on the floor

TWO
The Approach to the Problem

Aisha hadn't awakened by the time Alec decided to go out, so he left a note promising he'd be back soon. He got in his car and drove to a mall he'd seen the day before—only ten minutes from her house. He walked in, shuffled around his pocket for some change, remembered his calling card so pulled it out and dialed. It was answered on the third ring.

"It's Alec. Did I wake you?"

There was hesitation before an answer. "No."

"Is Billy there?"

"I just got back from taking him to school."

He shuffled in place, jammed his free hand into his pocket. "How are you?"

"We're fine."

"How are *you*?" he asked again.

She sighed. "I'm doing okay."

"I'm sending out the check today."

He heard a snicker on the other end and waited. "If you need anything, any of you," he began again.

She cut him off. "Billy needs a father, Alec. Why'd you call today?"

He sighed again. He was too young to feel this way, too young to experience this activity always reserved in the movies for some paunch, balding forty-year-old. He wasn't even thirty, in the greatest shape of his life, and too young.

"I got tired of calling only on holidays or birthdays or special occasions." He was tired of more than that. He was tired of passing through town and staying in a hotel just to take his son to the park for a few hours, or buy him an ice-cream cone.

"You never signed the papers."

The discussion of the papers had been three months prior, over three phone calls climaxing with a visit where he was to meet her and Billy and sign. He met them—that day he couldn't play hard, his stomach knotted as it was—and he and Lisa talked. But he saw no papers. She had said she would send them.

"You never sent them," he reminded her.

The conversation lulled. He closed with an admission that he thought about them often, and she iterated the same. He asked if he could call again and she said whenever he wanted, or even come down.

"Are you sure?" he asked, feeling nervous.

"No one will have a problem with you wanting to see your son and your…" she cut herself off. He said goodbye and she did too, her voice soft. They hung up at the same time.

He walked to a soda fountain, paid seventy-five cents for a bottle of water, and drank it sitting in a wooden chair in the seating area between all the mall food outlets. He kept his mind empty. When he was done he tossed the bottle away, then got in his car and drove back to Aisha's house. She was up, sipping on a cup of coffee and sighed as he walked through the door.

"I thought you'd left for good."

He shook his head. "I always come back." He moved to the cabinet, pulled a cup for himself, and added, "I left a note."

"Doesn't mean you'd come back."

Alec sat across from her, taking a moment to take her in before sipping his coffee. He explained to her what he had surmised thus far, but he didn't know what it was her mother was looking for. He told her his idea, and as it turned out, it was the longest case he had ever worked.

DAY ONE:

They started things out the only way they knew how, the first full day of the case. They cleaned. They swept and mopped and did laundry and dishes and removed stains and swept cobwebs and dusted, and by the afternoon the downstairs was in order. Alec helped her carry the cleaning supplies up the stairs, and they sat everything down in the hall to survey what lay ahead of them. He felt her eyes on him as he turned to the bedroom door, touched the knob, shivered from its chill, and tried to open it. He sighed and hung his head.

"It's locked."

He heard the doubt in her voice when she spoke. "There are a lot of you guys out there, hunting for ghosts. What makes you think you can give them peace?"

He sighed again and wondered also, her question that he had asked himself many times. He thought of home, of what he left behind, and of what they had awakened seven years ago—five college kids out for an adventure, not meaning to wake anything. He snatched up the mop and soapy water, turned down the hall and took a step.

"Because I know what it's like to be haunted," he said, and it was the best answer he always gave, to why he always succeeded.

They began to clean.

DAY TWO:

He sat in defeat, staring at the cobwebs. The wine stain had reappeared, a ring on the coffee table embedded in the wood surface. He wiped the dust off a shelf and walked back into the kitchen, where the perturbed spirit had shattered a few dishes, in retaliation to the exercises of the previous day. Leaning on the counter, he watched her pick up the fragments. Milk had leaked from the fridge to a curdled puddle on the linoleum tiles. He was at a loss.

Her mother obviously in search of something, she must know they were trying to help. So why was she keeping the door locked? To that he couldn't formulate an answer. He looked around, asked himself why she was keeping the house in filth, and couldn't understand that either. He asked Aisha the cleaning habits of her mother while she was alive, and Aisha said they were meticulous, until the disease set in.

She stood and wiped off her pants. "Towards the end I had to have help in the house. I cleaned and cleaned and the woman—and it wasn't her fault, I know—but things always got messed up. It got to be all I could do to keep her sheets cleaned, and it took me and the nurse to change her." He detected bitterness in Aisha's voice, saw the curl in her lip and realized that was the first time she showed animosity for her mother. He didn't like the look, the sound, and wanted to reassure her that her mother was suffering probably worse than she was. He didn't, realizing as he watched her pace slowly with hands on hips, elbows back, that she was angry at the disease, not the woman.

DAY THREE:

Night fell, and the return to disorder after their futile day of cleaning was not a peaceful experience. They heard it all. They heard screaming, and trapped in her bedroom, Alec holding her and rocking her gently as she cried, they listened to the sound of a woman screaming in either anger or frustration, as things shattered and the house shook. Several times came a knocking at the door, and the screams sounded just outside, and Alec listened to Aisha scream back and tried to shush her, rocking ever slowly, himself silent and praying the locked door would hold and whatever had come to be that could scream like that would not enter the room. He didn't want to see it. It never entered, and he thought of the locked door, and another idea began to work itself into his mind. But it was one he wasn't ready to vocalize just yet. All today the door was locked, as it had been, and now as he held her he could hear footsteps leave her door, walk to the locked bedroom. He heard that door open and slam shut and sounds of thrashing in there and chaos. The door opened again and he heard footsteps along the stairs, and he knew that soon the downstairs would echo with the chaos and then it would be back at their door, beating on it. And always screaming.

DAY FOUR:

He used a Phillips nimbly, handing each screw to Aisha as he removed it, sure now about his new idea. He had one hinge to go, and then the door would not be hung on the frame. It would be loose, and they would be able to get into the bedroom. Listening and watching, he had formulated this new theory, but had yet to voice it to Aisha. He wasn't sure how she would accept it, such an idea of another spirit causing the disturbances in the home? He wasn't sure. Several nights so far, as the activity worsened throughout the night, Aisha had seemed on the brink of collapse—breakdown, his mind interjected—and such new information might do more to frighten her than help right now.

The last hinge pulled free, and the door gave to the floor. He smiled to himself, felt his shoulders swell, and forced himself not to look at Aisha. They were about to enter, and though that was the goal, what was inside might prove more disturbing than they had thought. Something obviously didn't want them in there, and he had—for that reason—to keep his emotions in check. At least until they were sure.

He gripped the knob—still like ice—and reached his other hand for the door's edge, searching for a grip to pull it free. He thought he found one and tugged. The door held. It stood secure against his best pull, his muscles tensed, and he had to step away and look at it, study it. There should be nothing to hold it now. The lock securing it was old and not strong enough to keep the door braced against the frame. Unless the frame had swelled, he reasoned to himself. He tried again, then stepped back and shook his head. The door still wasn't going to give. Alec's eyes narrowed to slits, studying the door for weak points, and determination smoldered within. Soon his resolve would be up, and he'd wait. Just one more day and they'd try to clean again, and tomorrow, before Aisha woke…

DAY FIVE:

His shoulder connected with the door again; his eyes winced and he groaned. The door had barely shaken. He stepped back and looked around. Dawn was settling on the house, and soon Aisha would be up, and he wondered if she'd be angry that he was trying to bust down the door. He could afford to buy her another one, he realized. He was the ghost hunter. His colleagues were busy trying to document the existence of ghosts, or use mediums and special gadgets to determine their locality and to help them to rest, forgetting all the while that ultimately they are people. But he was the ghost hunter, and by God and fury he got the job done, no matter the cost, because he treated them as people. Something reminded him of his own ghosts, and he ignored it, because they weren't the problem at hand. His shoulder slapped the face of the door again, and he stopped, ear against it, listening to breathing from the other side. The door had given more, and he reminded himself they were just people. Just people that were lost now; he stepped back, ran, dug his shoulder in and the door fell inward. Alec caught himself, looked up and found he couldn't move.

Ghosts were more than that; ghosts were people that should no longer be. That's why, as Alec stared into the face of her father, dead eyes vacant yet so full of anger as its form hunkered to him with clenched fists, that's why he caught his breath. It screamed and rushed for him, and that's why Alec screamed in return.

She was examining a copy of her father's will, written about three years ago, notarized, giving strict specifications on every item, including Aisha. There were provisions that his wife couldn't negotiate her will in contradiction to his after his had been notarized, and if she had Aisha would lose everything. No matter what, Aisha and her mother would lose the cabin.

The house had quieted, and Alec watched her sitting on the bed, pouring over the paperwork, cursing under her breath. He stood by the window, staring out, thinking about what Lisa had said on the phone.

"What's the big deal about that cabin, anyway?" he asked. He had spent way too long at this job, feeling things he shouldn't feel.

She told him her mother had grown up in that cabin; her parents had left it to her when they passed. Suddenly and tragically was all Aisha would say about that. Her mother and father took out a mortgage on the cabin when they were young to buy this house, to help them set up their life. When they paid it off, he just assumed he owned it. He never liked the cabin, she added with disgust, never liked it when the family took vacations there, but he did it to please Mom. She threw the paper down and stretched out on the bed, arms behind her head. She stared up at the ceiling, and Alec heard the house start up again.

The doorknob rattled viciously. The door like a bass drum as something pounded on it. Then the walls swelled and the house groaned. Pipes began humming, and Aisha began screaming from where she lay.

"They hated you! Didn't they, Dad? They saw you for who you were, and they hated you. That's why you didn't want us to have the cabin. You wanted to take everything about them away from us."

The house quieted. She sat up in bed, legs straight, arms bracing her up. Her chin touched her chest and she crumpled forward, hands covering her face. Sobs came quietly as slight tremors and whispers, and Alec sat next to her, holding her, rocking gently and shushing her, cursing himself for being here too long. Ghosts, he realized then, are a private matter, intimate and personal and outsiders like him or priests or psychics didn't belong. He rocked her till she quieted, then looked up. Darkness pervaded, and Alec felt like something was waiting. He felt as though he was being watched, a paranoid feeling surely, but the storm had subsided too quickly. He waited a few more minutes before standing, waved her off when she reached for him. He walked to the door, and with the slightest hesitation, pulled it open with a creak.

The hall was just like the room: dark, silent. He stepped out, his eyes searching, relief growing as he found nothing. He turned and walked down the hall to the room where she had seen something that first night, the room where the activity seemed to be centered. The door back on its hinges was shut, a little hot to the touch, and his hesitation was longer. The palm of his hand warmed as though he had touched a light bulb, but still he turned the knob. The door gave easy, and swung open. A breeze escaped, he quivered and stepped into the room and flicked on the light.

The welcome light showed him too much. The corner dresser had been overturned, the papers and linens it shelved strewn about the floor. The mattress had been flipped; its dressings rumpled and scattered. There were holes in the wall, and he imagined such frustration at whatever she was searching for, that she must have lashed out, punched something. The door to the closet had been opened, and for all the light given to the room, the closet was black. He stepped toward it, and as he moved, slowly, he began to hear something. It sounded at first like Aisha; he shook his head. It wasn't. It was a voice, not in his ear but penetrating his head, whispering for him to go home. It said he was tired, he needed to sleep, and after he slept he needed to go home.

He pushed the door closed, and that's when the world left him, because that's when the voice told him to do something, before he left for home and after he slept. That's also when he caught a glimpse of her mother, the head just over his shoulder, leaning over, her lips just moving. "Find it," she said, and then he collapsed. He was just aware of the room swirling as he fell to the floor.

THREE

Resolutions

He is back in school, rushing from building to building, first trapped in the north tower of Old Main, then getting to Kimple Hall, then to the student union and next door bus station. It is the last day of finals, and he can't find Lisa. He nearly runs, pushing his way through a crowd that seems to impede him no matter where he is. He feels something, always at the corner, watching him, trailing him, and he knows if he doesn't find her, he'll never see her again. Just to see her one last time, but she isn't who he finds first.

His mother sits at a long oak table in a high-back chair, in the middle of the union. Around this table is his family. The people walking by all take a casual notice before turning lurid eyes away. No one blinks.

A chair is waiting for him. His family is the color of silverfish, their dark eyes sunken and locked to the surface of the table.

"I'm scared."

His mother looks at him. "Find her again."

"I'm trying," he tells her.

"Bullshit," his father says, "you know where she is."

"I don't." He shifts in his seat, looks at the passers-by.

"You've got to do right by your family," his grandfather says. Alec starts to say he was trying, but he hangs his head.

"Where are you?" he asks. He knows the answer. They are where he should be, and he stands and walks out of the union, passes the fountain heading toward the library. Only the library isn't there anymore. The wide marble steps lead up to an A-frame house, two stories with a balcony over the stone porch. It is wooden, a

mimosa tree in bloom to the left, a patch of irises on the right and a lilac bush at each front corner. A mockingbird sings to him from the mimosa, and bumblebees float over the stone walk like sentries guarding the path. Clouds build up behind the house, and the window upstairs gives off a red light. Wind tousles his hair and the clouds darken everything, chasing off the sentries and wilting the blooms. As it begins to rain he tears his gaze away from the house's eyes. The front door opens. Lisa and the kids file out. A lanky man with red hair emerges, dragging the limp body of Alec's younger brother by the scalp, blood up to the redhead man's elbow. The redheaded man is smiling.

He opened his eyes to Aisha hovering over him. His shirt was off, a cool rag moistening his chest, driven by Aisha's hand. He tried to smile, but breath was hard, and he saw in her eyes a softness that he felt wrong to try and reciprocate. Dust particles danced in golden light, drifting through the blinds of her room, and when he asked what time it was, she said it was after noon. He stretched then yawned, and his body swelled. Aisha asked what happened.

"I collapsed from exhaustion," he said. She just looked at him. "I don't sleep much anymore," he explained.

Despite her protests, he rose and pulled away from her. He followed her downstairs to the kitchen, watched as she fixed lunch and drank four glasses of water.

They didn't talk throughout the afternoon about the house or her mother. Instead Alec turned the topic to a more personal nature as they sat on the couch. The television was off. Their eyes were locked. His hand had moved unconsciously to hers, both resting on her bare thigh. Even that felt wrong. She wore shorts, and his curled fingers were able to feel her soft flesh, an intimate touch that, while innocent, secretly excited him. The touch also made him tremble and question himself, morally. She didn't seem to mind.

"You're beautiful," he said, and wondered if it came out too tender.

"Why don't you have a boyfriend, a husband?"

She shrugged and looked away. "I don't know. I just haven't found the right guy." She looked at him. He felt as though he was back in high school, as he smiled at her and she returned it. He felt her squeeze his hand.

"Can I take a shower?"

She nodded.

It was nearly dark as the water cleansed him; he smiled and continued to lather. His thoughts were jumbled; his mind focused on many things. Her form, especially as she was hovering over him when he awoke—he never thought to ask how he made it back to her bed— her hand touching his chest with a cool rag. His shoes had been off, and he had felt the instep of her bare foot rubbing against his. He sweat under the shower then caught his breath and thought of the house, what her mother must be searching for. He knew there must be something to override the will of Aisha's father, but he couldn't begin to guess where to find it, or what it could be. Fantasy filled him then; he rinsed his body and shampooed his hair again. He'd find what he needed, what Aisha needed, and she'd be so grateful, and ask him to stay, and he'd get a second chance to do it right. And this time he wouldn't run.

He thought of the voice, what it whispered, the room just down the hall where he had heard it before falling asleep. The overturned dresser in the corner, linens and paper scattered about, littering the floor…he jumped out of the shower.

Barely giving himself time to wrap the towel about his body, he rushed from her bathroom, passed her lounging on her bed examining her father's will again, and rushed to the other room. It was silent, and the sun had fallen considerably. He heard her first, then felt Aisha's touch on his shoulder, as she stood just behind him, whispering what was wrong.

He blew a tuft of wet hair out of his eye and stared into the darkening room. Somewhere deep inside the house, he could hear the noises start again.

The top drawer to the bureau by the wall was open. He whispered her name, asked her who owned that and she said her mother. He walked over and began looking through it. An envelope had fallen between the crack in the back of the drawer, so much that barely a corner was visible. He was afraid he'd have to muscle the backing off to pull it out, but that wasn't the case. Snagging the corner he pulled, let off for fear of tearing it, pulled again.

It came free. He opened the envelope and saw a notary seal dated three months before her father's will. *Just as her mother was diagnosed*, he thought, *just before her father died*. His smile sang as an erupting laugh to which she jumped.

He asked her to verify the date on her father's will, and began to read. This one had come first. He began to smile, rushed to the desk and flicked on the reading light, his smile broadening. He laughed out, called her over and showed the document to her. They were both laughing, she nearly in tears. They hugged and agreed that she should call her attorney the first thing the next morning. He asked what had happened to the cabin and she said it had been on the market, and it might have a buyer now. He said she could take it off the market, if she liked. She hugged him again, stared into his blue eyes, kissed him.

He didn't return the kiss.

Alec stepped back, surveyed her, even caressed her cheek. But when she reached for him, he pulled away and shook his head. His gaze dropped to the floor and he breathed a sigh. When he looked at her he offered a smile, and spoke slowly.

"I can't." It was all he could say. He had his reasons, but where he should have explained himself, he couldn't. He lowered his eyes again, thought of how beautiful she was and let the fantasy play in his head.

"Will you stay?" she asked. "Can you at least stay?"

"I'll sleep downstairs."

She shook her head. "Hold me."

He did manage that.

Alec woke up. Blue light cast a dim glow on everything. He inched out of bed so as not to wake her and walked downstairs to start a pot of coffee. Echoes of dreams haunted him.

His legs trembled underneath him as he walked. He collapsed at the kitchen table, sipping at the cup. Sick and trembling, he realized he had never mourned the deaths of his family. He had spent the last six months chasing ghosts, helping others. He looked about the room. Aisha entered, wearing her own robe, her thighs revealing themselves with every step. She sat next to him with her own cup of coffee, staring at him, trying to smile but he could see she was nervous. He reached for her hand in an attempt to console her, to try and explain why he couldn't stay, but words were futile and in the end he could only say one thing.

"*Hacimos ruidos por la noche.*"

Lisa had dreamed also. But her dream had left her confused. She sat up in bed and simply breathed, recalling all she had experienced, realizing that she had done more than dream. She had a conversation, with someone who, by all scientific rights, should not be able to communicate. She had talked to her niece's mother—Justine.

She needed caffeine. A vague interior voice tried to stall the onslaught of memories of the night's meeting: There was a time when you didn't need coffee.

They sat on the couch in the living room, and in the dream they were drinking coffee. The voice asked her if her life had become so boring that she even dreamed about ingesting something to keep her awake; she quickly retorted that her life was not boring. Justine was asking her about life in general, how things were going, how the kids were. When Lisa answered she expressed how Kimber was doing, especially.

"I miss her," Justine said, casting her eyes down, a smile waning.

"I know," Lisa answered.

Justine kept up the small talk, long after it had worn thin. Lisa knew her friend well, and asked her what was wrong.

"Thinking about the past," Justine answered, the expression on her face as vague as her answer. "Thinking about what is coming."

"You heard me tell Alec he could come back anytime?" Lisa knew she had; *they* heard everything.

"You miss him."

"There's still a lot of anger there," Lisa said. "We both have a lot of resentment."

"You still love him."

Lisa shrugged, and realized she couldn't even repeat the word. Maybe all that anger did harbor latent, softer emotions. Maybe the anger played off the fact that love was still there, and the angry part of her just wanted all that to be gone. It was some form of catch-twenty-two, or something like that—maybe just some pop-psychology she had heard and decided to accept.

"I was thinking about how scared I was that night," Justine was saying. Lisa didn't need clarification. She knew to which night her friend was referring. "And you made it all sound so logical, I almost wasn't scared anymore."

"Until the mirrors shattered," Lisa added. "Then I think we all were scared."

"We let them out. Did you ever wonder where Karl went?"

Lisa nodded. Alec had told her about his visit with his one-time friend, and what he had learned about Karl's whereabouts that night. Lisa herself had visited him once since that night, and she had told Alec about it, and he wasn't happy about it. He had been more worried about her. Lisa told her friend where Karl had been.

"Do you think he'll be there for good?"

Lisa didn't think so. She shook her head, sipped her coffee and didn't like where this was going.

"He'll get out," Justine said matter-of-factly. "They'll bring him back here."

"I know," Lisa said, her voice small.

"Can you protect those kids, all by yourself?" Justine gave her only minimal time to answer. "Even if you could, could you do it and survive? What would it cost you?"

"It would be easier if Alec were here," Lisa admitted.

"Not just here," Justine said, looking around. She reached out, and with a single finger she touched Lisa's chest, and Lisa then awoke.

She could hear the children stirring. She would have to ready them without her morning pot of coffee. She tried to tell herself that it was all a moot point, that Alec wasn't here and he wouldn't take her suggestion to come, and so nothing her friend had said—not her friend, but the manifestation of her conscience as her deceased friend—mattered. For the rest of the day and through the next night, she found she was at odds with herself.

FOUR

The Haunted Man

The first year Karl wasn't used to bouncing around. There was a part of him that knew it all necessary; things had gone terribly wrong, and they had awakened something and now he was paying for it. The rehab center of Pulaski County cleansed his body of the drugs—his only crutch for dealing with what he saw—and then he was sent to lockdown. The visions came quickly as his body was purified, and as he saw more of them, the director felt it best to put him in lockdown. He stayed on the seventh floor of the Pulaski County Regional Hospital for three weeks—the longest they could hold him—as the doctor tried to convince him that they weren't real. He begged them not to let him sleep in the dark at night, because that's when the shadowfolk came and spoke to him. To listen to them was like seeing them, mere glimpses of whispers, and the sight of them, silhouettes with eyes as red as the sky at dusk, hollowed him, their own eyes hollow and veiling the coming darkness. The medical professionals sent him to a halfway house next; he wasn't a danger to anyone, just a poor soul tormented. His first day there he checked in, was told of a job where he could make a little money, applied and on his way back picked up some weed. The house director smelled it, found the resin coated pipe and had him sent back to rehab.

The second year, things improved little. His college buddy came and visited him once, and Lisa came. That was his saving grace, seeing her again. They told him what she was carrying before she was showing.

They could sense it, like animals on the hunt. That's what they were to him, animals divested of form, using him to get to their food. Lisa was with his college buddy's child, and they knew it probably before she did. That's what they wanted.

The third year came and passed, bouncing still from rehab to the halfway house when they found drugs, and back to the lockdown unit when sobriety let the shadowfolk in too much, leaving him screaming in the middle of the night. He was haggard, his eyes red-rimmed, his cheeks sagging. He found some meth once and almost found the time shoot up before they caught him.

The fourth year he wished for solace from friends, to see his old college buddy again or Alec's wife, Lisa. He especially wanted to see Lisa. God if Alec hadn't bitched things up for him, Lisa would be his. That was what they were willing to give him, if he only put up with them a little longer. But they were relentless, and he couldn't access release from them. The only way he got through the fourth year of this epoch of his life was with the thoughts of Lisa and the promises of spirits unrelenting.

The fifth year set him back. He was caught three times with pot, and twice with cocaine. He spent most of his time in rehab, and twice was sent straight from there to the lockdown unit. The doctor looked exasperated as she walked into the room, welcoming him with a thin smile. He paid little mind. The lights were on and the shadowfolk were only whispers.

"I need the drugs," he said. "The drugs keep them away."

"You still see them?" she asked. It was a stupid question, he knew, but she was trying to get the ball rolling.

"Put me away someplace. Lock me away. Just don't keep bouncing me around like this."

"You know we can't lock you away."

He felt himself go wild, stand and began to rant, "I will. I'll kill someone. I'll kill you. If you let me out of here, I'll kill you first." And for all the flailing of his arms and loudness and exaggerated movements, he didn't believe it. He couldn't convince himself of that so he sank down and put his head between his knees. "Just lock me away and keep me sedated. Let me have some rest."

She watched him. He could feel her eyes on him, saw the sympathy; she hadn't believed his threat either.

"I want to kill myself."

They were reluctant to send him back to the halfway house at the end of that three-week tenure.

The sixth year slowed, and he spent more time at the halfway house than ever before. He still saw them, still heard them, and he had a few slips. But things were changing. He couldn't know that seven years after their awakening, seven years after bouncing around in search of normalcy, he'd be released. And then all the promises made would be kept, and both he and the shadowfolk would get a chance at the things they most wanted.

Alec would lose it all.

He remembered the first time he met Alec; a boy a few years younger than he, soft around the middle, a hopeless romantic with every action, every notion in his own philosophy. Convinced as Alec was that his drinking was a problem, it took Karl some work to get him out to the bars, but once there Alec needed little coaxing. He was weak, and all of this Karl saw the first day he met Alec.

⁂

The professor is talking as Karl approaches the door opened to a crack. He just sees the professor's face, a wrinkled man with salt-and-pepper hair sporadically dyed brown and a beak nose and large, round eyes. Their conversation—whoever the professor is talking to, he must be talking to someone—has just begun, and after a brief knock and a motion from the professor Karl enters and sees Alec Bradshaw.

The professor makes the introductions. Alec is a junior in the English program, taking the professor's Intro to Philosophy as a requirement. Karl—the professor beams—is a philosophy major, and he speaks so that Karl blushes. Alec is formal with pleasantries, even shakes Karl's hand and offers a smile. He seems a little uneasy about sitting in the office.

"He wants to know my philosophy on God," the professor explains to Karl.

Alec explains his side: that every class they have, no matter which philosopher they are discussing, or which ideal of morality, it always leads back to a Sunday School sermon with the devout chastising the intellectuals with half-logical arguments, and the devil's advocates in the center egging both sides on. The intellectuals, Alec reasons, aren't so much that as debunkers hiding behind the guise of reason, and come off more attacking the devout than trying to reason the existence of God. All of them are undergraduates, still infants in learning, with a lack of experience that can only clutter issues more reasonably tackled by learned men.

"You're looking for the truth," the professor exclaimed, nodding.

"I seek the opinion of someone with more experience at using the tools you are just now giving us."

Karl listens, silent. Alec, for what it's worth, is a handsome man, no blemishes, no features out of sync, and intelligent. But there is hunger in his eyes, a green hunger tainted red with hope and love and romantic ideals of everything, including God.

"I see God as the watchmaker," the professor begins, and explains that theory of a creator who has long since abandoned his creation. "But I think He does watch."

"How can he see everything?" Alec asks, nearly to himself. The professor has an answer for that also.

"Imagine a tall cliff, and at the base a river flows to a bend right where the cliff disappears into the water. There are three canoes on that river, and from His vantage point God can see them all. An hour up-river floats one canoe, another is at the base, and an hour down-river floats another. From the top of the cliff all can be seen, but from each canoe the others are not visible. The canoe up-river cannot see the one that is an hour passed the bend; neither can the one just making the bend. But the man on the cliff can see all of them, as well as the rapids, the sloughs, the rocks and the calm areas."

"But he can't reach them to intercede," Alec says, nodding.

He is also gullible, Karl thinks.

His lips curled at that day, and he realized again Alec didn't deserve what he had received. But all that would change soon, and that made him smile. He was the rock, unseen by the canoe about to round the bend at the base of the cliff, and nothing was going to stop him.

It had all come together nicely, he realized. He saw them.

They swarmed, they hovered over him, and out of the corner of his eye he caught one, passing through the crack at the door. Another appeared just behind his shoulder, a whisper he felt and heard, as their red eyes peered down on them. And then, their voices one shallow hum, like a bee swarming down to sting, they began to speak to him. They filled his mind with images and sounds and reminders of the noises a soul made when they devoured it. It was indescribable and awful, the worst thing he had ever heard. Nothing alive could make that sound, because these things were already dead, when they began to eat, and the sound was of something crying as it was slowly masticated out of existence. After the shadowfolk, there was no Heaven or Hell. There was nowhere a spirit could run, because they had come to the end. He marveled at them, then, even as they ravaged him, seduced him, tortured him. He marveled as they infected his mind and soul and promised him things, if he would just help them. In his diseased state he marveled, and for him they were more powerful than God or Satan, even as he screamed.

There were drugs, then, to quiet him, and people there who didn't realize in what presence they stood. Of course they are powerful, he whispered, staring blankly up at their sanguine eyes, ignoring the people trying to quiet him. His eyes, unseeing, were wide with awe. They were, after all, responsible for all that had happened. He felt sure they had brought him and Alec together in the professor's office, that day. They had been along—somehow—when Alec first introduced him to Lisa. They birthed the interest in the boys for spirits, that would give way to their own union with him on a road trip. They had brought it together just fine. It had taken all this time, but he finally began to realize just how powerful they were.

Keys jangle in Alec's hand, and he looks around nervously. The street is dark, cool, noises drawing the people down the way toward the bars, and away from the used bookstore on the corner. Karl isn't sure why Alec is so jumpy; no one will suspect anything. Alec works here, he comes and goes all the time and can, for at least thirty hours a week, be found inside this store. Maybe after closing time he has just forgot something.

The heavy glass door swings inward, and Alec ushers him in. They step past a wood cart sheltering paperbacks, into a musty room encompassing leather bindings and old cloth bindings, with powdery, jaundicing leafs in between. Alec breathes in as though he were an urbanite stepping for the first time into the much-anticipated country air. Karl looks around and sees some gilded books. He appreciates the beauty of this place, and finds the knick-knacks scattered about gild the room.

He saw their eyes—the drugs didn't sedate him enough—and wondered what gilded their vision so, against children and spirits.

"There is a ghost here," Alec had said while they still sat at the bar, sipping beer.

Karl looks around the room. High shelves reach upward, way over his head, and are filled to capacity with books, and to the back are other rooms, divided into a labyrinth by shelves filled with titles.

Up the ramp they find the section on the occult, read some ghost stories and explore the locked rooms that are poorly lit, just as segregated as the customer areas. These are filled with duplicate titles of the thousands of books already in view for the public. There are sounds in these rooms, and stagnant air that aches to be sighed again. There are sounds in the walls, and Karl remembers the story Alec told him, about the two present owners once having a third friend that still watches over the store, due to his love of books.

They had spent two hours in the store that night, and never saw anything. But it had been exciting. It had been mysterious. It had been every reason people flock to graveyards or reputed haunted houses. It was the reason that, even when nothing had been seen, people went back. Because it was something that was felt, every time. It was a door to the mysterious, a door to the past, and when the shadowfolk showed themselves to Karl, in their little prison in South Arkansas, it was the only door that seemed logical to open.

As the drugs took effect, he smiled at all they had done for him. People watching would undoubtedly be concerned, such ravings followed by such a content sleep. But Karl was happy. The attacks were brief—and horrifying—but easily overshadowed in what they could do, what they would bring. He had done right, when he had suggested the road trip.

FIVE
Reggie Val and the Little Girl

Alec popped the cap off the bottle and put two more quarters in the Magic Fingers at the head of his bed. He hadn't had a drink in seven years; he sucked the first one back without thought. The second led him deeper into his memories. He contemplated turning on the television, denied that idea, drank instead and thought of Aisha. He drank and thought of the ghosts. He began to wonder what Lisa was doing now, if the kids were in bed. Of course they were, he realized, and his mind stole him to another place.

First there were the howls at the old mill. It had been a cold night, the air as wet and chilled and full of intoxication as the bottle he gripped. He took another drink. An old man and his dog had been murdered one hundred years ago, and the dog was out, still seeking the killer. That was the story anyway. He didn't want to believe it until he heard the howls for himself, standing next to the sheriff, as the night blurred with mist. He shivered, remembering how scared he had been that night, the sheriff turning to him and saying in that thick Minnesota drawl, "The dog is coming." The wind carried the howl over the hills, through the grove of trees surrounding them; the wind tossed their raincoats. The sheriff clicked the hammer back on his shotgun.

At the time he was just driving north to get away. He had heard what was going on and decided to help. They were hesitant, first, then grateful. The sheriff told him his brother was having problems in Ohio; he lived on the family farm with his wife and kids.

From there, on a whim—and for the two jobs Alec had been paid well, he had saved lives—he posted his jobs on the Internet. He left and visited the kids and talked to Lisa. There was still a lot of resentment, and neither had an answer as to what was going to happen. He left abruptly when he got word of a plantation in Louisiana, just north of New Orleans. The Cajun State provided him with some of the worst scares he had seen, and he found that spirits could be violent creatures. He also caught a reminder of something that had chased them, years ago.

On the Mississippi River he found a riverboat and his next job, and he was anxious to escape the plantation. He also found an old black woman, living in a shack; it felt like years ago now. Ancient mariners cried nightly about atrocities they once faced, that killed them but wouldn't let them pass.

Then there came a lull. He took the break to visit Lisa about some papers, which he never saw, and from there he drove back to where it all began. In Reeder, Arkansas, underneath the pines, he stopped to look at the house. In the seven years it had fallen more, wasn't even accessible. He started to walk away, his car still parked in front of the house, and then he turned around and went back to it. It would be safer not to leave it there, because it was going to be dark soon. He drove down the road to the railroad crossing, waited until nightfall, remembering the story he had heard since he was a child.

He looked across the room to the mirror, stretching over the dresser. He didn't like the way he looked after he had downed a few. He pulled another out from the mini-fridge by the bed, popped the top and realized he wouldn't like how he'd feel tomorrow morning. He had lied to Aisha, when she asked if the shadowfolk had ever gotten a child.

The car door opens, and Alec Bradshaw steps onto Georgia soil. From behind his shades he examines the Victorian plantation house, the oaks shading the yard, the field houses just behind and the forest in the distance. On the porch stands a bald man with a gray suit and black cowboy boots, smoking a cigarette. The man saunters up to Alec who, removing his shades, offers a hand to the man in boots. He looks up to the house, and out of the corner of his eye Alec sees a badge catch rays of the sun.

"Where is she?" Alec asks.

The detective points to the house, to the second floor. "Damn lucky you were so close. I've never seen anything like this."

Alec nods. He looked up to the shuttered window with drapes pulled closed. He has just come from Endsville, Mississippi, and had stopped at Moorshead, twenty miles south, for gas. He asks when the M.E. is due. The detective says he is on his way, stuck at the courthouse at the county seat about fifteen miles from here, and just now leaving.

"You want to see her?"

Alec doesn't have to nod, just follows the detective up the steps and through the front door. The house is decorated much as he anticipated, remaining in the antebellum style of the nineteenth century, with high-back, wooden chairs, lavish white drapes, couches and love seats clothed in flower patterns, sitting on oak legs carved like hooves. No television can be seen, and Alec guesses the family saves such modern eyesores for less public rooms in the house. An old rotary phone sits on a high corner table; he wonders if it works. From just inside the door he can see three rooms and the wide stairs curving up to the second floor. Past the marble-floored foyer is the living room, painted and decorated in light blue. To his right is the dining room, a creamy pastel, and to his left is the sitting room, soft pink and orange trimmed in crimson. The rooms are individual, yet so subtle in their décor that they don't widely contrast each other; the pallet flows smoothly as his eyes survey the lower story. He takes special notice of the sitting room, because as empty as the rest of the house seems, this room is full. Twelve people sit around—a few stand because of lack of chairs— and Alec notices two things. Everyone is in a state of discomposure. Some cry, some rock, some look as though they are going to be ill. Others, including the man he concludes to be the family doctor, stare blankly ahead, gray pallor, unmoving— petrified. Of all of them, the cop resembles the last group the most.

"The family," the detective says, and gives a knowing look to Alec.

Alec asks where the girl is in a hushed tone, looking around for family reactions.

"Upstairs," the cop whispers back.

The mother looks up. She is some cross between ill and sobbing, her face taking on both tones—red and green—her eyes puffed, her whole body shaking. She stands, walks up to Alec, grabs his collar, then wraps her arms around him. He tries to comfort her, barely knowing the situation, not knowing what to say, patting her back, until she pulls away and grabs his collar again.

"You're just a kid," she says.

He smiles, consoling.

"The screams," she says, then looks around. "We have no ghosts here, anymore." Her vacant eyes stare past him, and with a blink her mood changes. She pushes away, stares at the detective, her eyes dark and wild. "No! We have no ghosts. They devoured the ghosts." Something about the way she says that unsettles Alec—he has heard it worded such a way before. "And then they took her."

Alec asks who, and she looks at him as though that is the simplest question of all. She cocks her head to one side, examines him. She brushes past him and takes his hand, tugs at him till he follows. He catches a glimpse of her face as she passes; sees her unblinking eyes, her head still cocked. She leads him up the stairs. He can hear the detective following; feels her grip, cold and rough, like ground soil in December. She leads him through the upstairs hall, pushes open the door, leads him in right to the bed. He has no time to acknowledge the stench, like hell has vented into the room, nor the chill. He is looking at the girl.

Curled into the fetal position, her back to them, still dressed in her nightgown, she looks as though she had been dead for thousands of years, and just removed from her tomb and unwrapped. He kneels, trying to close off his nostrils without lifting his hands, staring at the cracked shell. He bends over her, touches her shoulder gently as what was skin powders the tip of his finger, sees the eyes are only dark hollows. He straightens.

"She had been sick for sometime," the mother says.

Alec stares.

"Of course they were already here."

There is a calmness in the woman's voice that unnerves him; he looks to the detective who—no stranger to this—is starting to look ill. The mother says they had found the covers over the girl, and her voice trembles. She bites at her nail, her vacant stare directed to some point on the bed. She adds the covers were covering her baby's head, still trembling, still biting her nail.

"Like she was hiding."

He knows the sight of the little girl will bring many sleepless nights. They leave *the driveway and turn onto the highway, driving awhile, not speaking. Alec doesn't know where the detective is taking him, even as the car turns down a dirt road and Alec notices the worn shocks. They stop at a rundown cabin, where a man in rags sits hunched over on the porch, holding a beer can in one head. The man, the detective says, is Reginald Valentine, "Reggie Val" to the locals. Alec takes another look.*

Reggie Val is scrawny, with a bit of a paunch around the middle, and has the appearance of being sway-backed even as he sits. Reggie, his face scruffy, takes a gander at them, then looks back to the hard ground beneath the rickety boards on his porch. Reggie Val, the detective continues, used to be the caretaker for them at the plantation home, until about six months ago, when they fired him. Alec asked why they fired him. Reggie said he found something, tells the detective. He said he found something on that property, something that should have stayed buried.

"He told us they were haunting him nightly. They tricked him, made him see things. He'd come in four and five times a week, sometimes, and sometimes we wouldn't see him for a week or two."

They leave the car and approach the steps. Reggie Val takes a good look at them, especially Alec.

"They gone, detective," Reggie Val says, still eyeballing Alec. "Who's this?"

"Alec Bradshaw. He believes in what you saw."

Reggie turns his eyes to the detective, pulls out a freshly rolled cigarette and lights it. "You do too, don't you. You seen the girl."

The detective starts to look away.

"How'd you do it?" Alec asks.

Reggie shakes his head, blows a puff of smoke at them. "I didn't. It was them. It was the shadowfolk." His voice changes, his gaze distant. "Like they just swirled around her, and sucked the life out of her. Like one of those meadow fogs in early fall, settles on the ground in the mornings, except this was black. And I see her screaming and kicking from under her covers—she thought she could hide from them, but they seen her all the same—and it's like someone let the air out of a balloon, everything just shriveled up. Only it didn't sound that way. It sounded worse, worse than when they found a ghost and ate it up."

"Why didn't you stop them?" Alec asks. Out of the corner of his eye, he sees the detective reach into his inner coat pocket.

"You can't stop them," Reggie snaps. He does something strange, aside from the change in his voice, that only Alec sees. He smiles and blinks and his eyes are lurid

—*not bloodshot. And not under the skin, but under the pigment of his skin, Alec sees a dark swirl.*

"Where's Reggie?" Alec asks. The detective is taken back; the thing in front of them smiles.

"He's been dead a long time," it says with voices deep and dark and echoing the words as they are spoken. "Since we took the girl. It feels like we've been free an eternity." It looks Alec up and down, smiling. "You're a smart one, Mr. Bradshaw. How's the wife and kids?"

Alec backs away and the detective pulls a gun. He shoots the thing that looks like Reggie Val between the eyes; the noise nor the action can release Alec from his state of shock. It falls dead, staring up at nothing, grinning. It doesn't bleed. It doesn't move. Alec wonders if the shot has killed it; he is afraid when the detective kneels. Blood begins to trickle from the hole and the detective tells him there is no pulse.

The detective stands by Alec again, both of them looking down at the body. "No one will come for him," the detective says. "He was sick."

They watch the body shrivel as black contrails bleed out and snake off the porch. They stand motionless, watching, unable to speak; Alec only thinks there must be another way to stop them.

Alec realized he was drunk for the first time in a long time, as he stood and swayed, the hotel room floor now the deck of a ship in tumultuous waves of inebriation. He clambered to the bathroom, first slamming into the wall then grabbing it, crawling along it. He splashed water in his face, heard a howl in the distance. He tried to push out the image of the little girl, found himself shaking uncontrollably. *Another beer will do it*, he thought, and he tried to walk back into the main room toward the fridge. He fell on the bed.

Dreams of his next stop came immediately—a century-old ghost roaming the halls of a private college in Central Arkansas—and at dawn Alec woke, showered off the grime, and did what he could to remove the taste from his mouth, like stale urine spiced. He recalled finishing the job, and there were closer jobs, as though something was calling him back to Rapps Barron, but he took Aisha's. He hadn't called them yet when he left Chicago headed southwest, entering Missouri and stopping just north of the city with the arch. Aisha had wanted him to stay, begged him. He pulled into a rest area—Aisha now four hours in his past—and allowed himself to remember the hardest thing.

He had left once before, seven years ago, because he was convinced his best friend had stabbed him in the back. He walked to the bathroom, relieved himself and got a bottle of water out of the machine. He sat on top a picnic table, his blond hair blowing in the wind, his tanned skin warming in the sun. He had been soft when he met Lisa.

Alec opened his eyes to a blue sky. Glancing over to the building with tourist information and restrooms and soda machines, he contemplated only the payphone. *She'd be home now*, he thought, then tossed the empty water bottle in the trash, pulled out his calling card and dialed. When she answered he asked immediately if she meant what he said, about coming back.

He smiled, sighed and hoped it didn't echo into the receiver. He told her where he was, then asked where the kids were. She had a meeting in about an hour at the school for next year's schedule; the kids were at daycare. Before he hung up, she offered a placated saying he found totally sincere coming from her lips.

"Have a safe trip."

THE FAMILY HOME

ONE

A Day's Drive

The nine-hour drive across Missouri allowed the intrusion of memories. Maybe it was hearing her voice again, or what he hoped to accomplish, but the memories centered on the mother of his son. Her eyes a color of green he had never seen before, so benefitting her skin tone whether it paled by winter or tanned from summer, all the more highlighted by her dark hair, curling to just below her shoulders. In the haze of early June—the temperature wasn't expected to break much higher than eighty—the horizon of green median blended with the blue sky; he saw the color for the first time since he had last looked into her eyes. He was returning to his grandfather's house, but he couldn't think of family. Meeting Lisa for the first time took such happier precedence. He knew, though, where such a memory would lead, and once he began reminiscing he wouldn't be able to stop, no matter how painful. Yes he had met her, and could never regret that. Yes he had married her, and he was now going home for a chance to rebuild that. But for a short time he had lost her, once, seven years ago, and that memory was always painful.

He drove south with radio off, the earth rolling under his wheels, and the memories began.

Alec sits on the back porch; Lisa is next to him, thigh to thigh, her small hands busy working the bowl of the pipe. She pulls out the lighter, sticks the pipe to her mouth and lights it. Then she passes it to him. The first round goes in silence like that, from Lisa to Alec and back, until she asks him if its cached and he says yes. She cleans it out and begins to pack it again. He's got a class coming up, but right now he doesn't care. He knows she has a few siblings and a blonde roommate— "she's the first natural blonde I've ever met", Lisa told him once—and she wants to be a teacher. He wants to know more.

"I took this great Philosophy class. It was an intro class, but you should take it if you have the chance. Ever had Dr. Evans?"

Alec shakes his head. He takes the pipe when she passes it and has to light it.

"I like black labs," she says, then inhales.

He smiles. "My parents have one."

"I know."

They pass it a few more times in silence, until she scoffs. That breaks his concentration—up until then his mind is beginning to race, his thoughts jumbled and incoherent—and he asks her what's up.

"My dad found my pouch the other day. It was 'marijuana' this and 'marijuana' that for like five minutes. He could have said ganja or weed or pot or bud or grass or anything—even dope."

"Just sounded preachy," he laughed.

"Yeah."

It's cached again, and she loads it for a third time.

"I want a lot of kids."

She begins telling him this and his mind, swimming, can't keep up. She wants kids and loves little kids and when she can't have anymore she'll adopt.

"All guys our age want is sex," he says, and wonders where that came from. He chances an arm around her and she accepts, hardly seems to notice in fact.

She gushes up to him. "All guys?"

He laughs.

"I just want to be held," she says, serious. "I hate it when guys just call when they want, but to be held is sometimes better than sex."

She goes on, he listens as best he can, until she decides the porch is dirty and she begins to sweep it off. She is frantic with the broom, cursing the bugs as they splatter on the concrete. He watches her sway, her hips swing and he smiles. Her back is to him. She turns and faces him, gushing again. "All clear."

They sit on the couch until her roommate comes home, watching The Price Is Right. *She splits a can of Dr. Pepper with him. A commercial comes on with a male model, shirtless, popping out of a lake, and she says she wants a guy like that. He knows she'll hug him when he leaves and hopes it is like the other hugs, with her arms around his neck and not his waist. The next commercial shows a buxom woman with shoulder length blonde hair and dark eyes. Lisa intimates that is probably his dream girl. He's too stoned to argue. One of the million thoughts is a hope that he can hold her one night, should she ever want him to.*

When Justine comes in, she plops on the other couch, throwing her purse and backpack on the floor. She is blonde with dark eyes, short and curved with tight fitting pants and a low cut shirt. Alec takes a glance but doesn't really notice. He can't look where he wants so he watches TV. Justine watches them, smiling, until he reminds Lisa that he has to get back to class.

Justine asks where his car is, and he says he left it at home. Lisa brought him over.

⁂

He had to stop just south of St. Louis and fill up the car with gas; that broke his road hypnosis. Alec felt like he had been sleeping, that groggy feeling that slowed his steps, forced out yawns, made his vision swim in a lightheaded sensation as he paid for gas and something to drink. He popped his back several times, shook his legs and tried to work out the stiffness. *Aging*—he thought as he groaned back into the driver's seat—*starts before thirty, when only a few hours straight driving becomes unbearable.* He could remember staying up with Lisa all night long, watching the sunrise and feeling tired but still able to function. Seven years ago he could drive from northwest Arkansas to Austin, Texas, without stopping, arriving earlier than expected and still have energy. It felt so long ago. He still had a family then; he and Lisa still had their whole lives. But it wasn't just seven years ago; even when Lisa was pregnant they had done similar things.

The landscape began to change; flatlands started to wrinkle into what would become the Ozark Plateau. He could picture them already, especially in early summer, an endless ocean of green, calm, the waves of hills with rounded crests gently rocking the landscape. Just two hours to the east where they had gone to school, the eastern edge of the Plateau looked violent, and he could see the Boston Range with sharper ridges and steeper slopes, as though the tranquil sea was overcome by a torrent and at any second the hills would crash down, tossing everything about. What god or storm allowed such natural phenomena in such close proximity must have been the same that tore at his own life. That sentience must have defined the word friend, and then used that tool to isolate Alec.

"It was no god or storm," he could hear his grandfather saying, "It was just people." An image of his grandfather sprung to his mind then: shorter than Alec, just reaching five-ten in his hey-day and down to five-eight by the time Alec really knew him; he was a plump man with gray hair slicked back, an oval face with soft eyes, that didn't smile as much as they used to. And then came the memory.

It wasn't a single event, but a conglomeration of his most remembered times spent with his grandfather. The old man in his recliner, or joining the boys on the hearth, or sitting by them on a tree trunk or a dirt bank as they hunkered over a pond with poles dangling, waiting for a bite. The old man was talking; the boys were listening. He told them stories. Some were true, some maybe not so much, some were about his life as a young man and some were about his parents— all the stories were fascinating. Albert Bradshaw had the knack and a love for it, which is identified with most southerners, and so he became a good storyteller. He was raised in meager surroundings, had worked for all he had, had acquired it, through intelligence and his own sweat. Sometimes, as implied by his stories, his own sweat was joined by his blood.

Alec's grandmother was a tiny woman, and before her strokes that put her in the nursing home, he remembered how fast she was. She seemed to be always moving, always doing something. Her green eyes shining behind trifocals, whose lenses covered a third of her forehead and part of her cheeks. Knowing that Alec and family were coming—though they lived in the same town, so going to Grandma's could realistically be done before going to the grocery store or after paying bills—gave cause enough to create a four-course meal. It was always delicious. She had an angel's voice, he recalled, that had always been cracked with age. It was sweet in his memories, nonetheless, like an old record still playing. Alec's earliest memories were of sitting on her lap, or on Albert's lap, her voice carrying to his toddler ears.

You are my sunshine
My only sunshine
You make me happy
When skies are gray

He smiled, his mind held at that one memory until the road hypnosis faded, and his concentration was forced to break.

Springfield, Missouri lent itself to more gas, and a bathroom break that should have come two hours ago. He was making good time and beyond the memories, another part of him was excited. He played over the scene of that day when he thought he had lost Lisa, down to what they were wearing, the pain in his chest, the curtains blowing from the breeze that entered through a screen door. He saw the look on their faces, as though the ball was his to continue the game, and he had dropped it; forfeited. It was one way to alleviate the pressure on his bladder. But as he climbed back into the car his excitement was gone. He sat at the exit to the station, looking left, looking right. Home was right. Home where there were ghosts and a son and Lisa, who seven years ago invited his friend over without him, then called his bluff. He looked left. The first three lanes were clear; cars were stopped in the distance, waiting for a light change. The turn lane was clear. He looked right. Cars were coming but they were still far enough back he could make the turn. He could go and take another case, and if it was what she wanted, he'd call her and sign the papers. He knew it had to be what she wanted. She had showed him seven years ago with that simple action that she wasn't interested. She used the excuse of his mourning for family to sleep with another man, because it wasn't what she wanted. Cars from the right were close enough that he couldn't make the turn, but he could always double back. He turned right.

He had tried to be what she wanted, after the initial shock wore off. He spent ten weeks becoming what she had told him she wanted. He found a road to double back on, noticed the lateness in the afternoon, knew it was only a couple more hours to home. Something inside him tried to remind him of the dream, tried to remind him how happy she had been when he did come back, that it was more than Karl's trip and fall that brought her back to Alec. He blocked it away, missed the road and continued south. There would be another road. His heart had taken over; his head sunk and his eyes darkened. He had loved her. He had done something no man was willing to do anymore, because as he came to believe, love doesn't exist. Tolerance was all one needed, when they had security and lust to fuel them. Karl would be Billy's father, if he hadn't flipped. Not Alec, despite what he did seven years ago.

Now it was Alec's father—or rather his voice—that interjected, said, "Bullshit," and it was so loud in his mind that Alec literally turned in his seat to look around the car while driving. Nearly crossing to the next lane and the car occupying it, he corrected and straightened, and focused on the road ahead. His father's voice was right. It was bullshit to think that Karl would be in his shoes now, for two reasons. She did love him, and as Cory told him once, she did choose. She chose before Karl flipped.

He silently thanked his father and then prayed he wouldn't hear another voice, and then he thought of William Bradshaw. Hefty, like Albert, Alec's father came closer to reaching Alec's six-foot marker than his father before him, but still he came up short. His hair was thinning; he had a sedentary job and worked at it all the time. He was an intelligent man, a creative man, and used that combination to provide a service not usually found in a small town like Rapps Barron. He had been a success. But there was a part of him that could relate to Alec's more artistic nature, and his renaissance father understood when Alec came home downtrodden, after Karl had apparently swiped his girl, and his brother had become a turncoat. In a way that was both gruff and understanding, he had counseled Alec like he had been schooled in psychology, and understood Alec's pain. Artists, for better or worse, wear their heart on their sleeve—was the colloquialism his father had used. Every action, every response to what took place in daily life, was driven by an artist's emotions. That was what governed their creativity, and allowed them to seem more sensitive at times than most people.

"It bites," Alec scowled.

His father had nodded. "Yes. It does."

Recalling how his father looked the night Billy was born—unwell, tired, unaware that his time was nearly up—Alec found it juxtaposed against his mother's beaming face. She had always lived in the shadow of Alec's grandmother, and while she had always tried to compensate to the point of seeming overprotective, she never was bothered by the maternal success of his grandmother. No one had cared for the Bradshaw matriarch more than Alec's own mother, when the elder woman grew sick, unable to care for herself. No one could imagine how much she suffered, when they lowered Alec's father into the ground to sleep forever.

Dusk and Alec slowed on the country street two miles off the state highway. He looked right to a row of trees and shrubs, broken only by a gravel drive. No other car on the street and still he flicked on the blinker and turned. The gravel popped under the tires; the drive went straight, down a hill, or forked left in a semi-circle. He took the fork. Hedges lined the yard and drive; it was better visible from the lake two hundred feet below. The house was wooden, a three story A-frame with a balcony facing the front at the zenith of the A. He pulled around the semicircle, staring at the house, the stone fireplace on the left. Cubed off maple blocks, six-foot-long, served as steps down the left side of the hill, under the breakfast room balcony, and around back to the entrance to the basement. Hedges grew just under the bay windows of the front exposure; river rock formed a walkway across the grass to the porch with red-clay tile, walls of imported stone of varying sizes, roofed by the front balcony. He stepped on the porch—barely larger than a walk-in closet—a little swing held up to his right between the stone column and the outside wall, a couple of potted plants. He looked back and behind his car, at the crux where the stem and arm of the Y-drive intersected, a flowerbed of irises swayed in the zephyr of day's end. He looked back to the gray door, reached to the gold plated handle, pressed down on the door latch and felt it give. The door drug over the hardwood floor and Alec walked inside.

He stood in the entrance hall, the living room open on his left, an expansive, stone fireplace overshadowed by a wooden mantle decorated with his grandmother's hummels. The ceiling rose at an angle from above the fireplace, its highest point in the center of the home. A six-foot long support wall, less than a foot deep, cornered off the hall and obstructed his view of the dining room and the kitchen beyond. He saw the carpeted stair leading up just in front of him. From upstairs he could hear water running; the playful screams of two children echoed down to him. He stepped forward and looked to his right. Along the low ceiling wall of the entryway stood an old grandfather clock, an anniversary gift from his grandfather to his grandmother, that hadn't worked in years. As he surveyed what he could see of the first floor, everything seemed fresh and, dazed, he felt like he was new to see it, though nothing had been changed. Then she rounded the corner.

His first thought was her eyes. He had seen her sporadically over the past six months, but never in the family home. Here, in a white t-shirt and red shorts, standing and staring at him with those eyes, he realized she hadn't changed. She still looked the same. A dishtowel she had crumpled between her fingers unfolded and draped to the floor. She didn't blink. He tried to smile and felt a click in his throat. She lowered her eyes then looked back up at him, and then she turned away.

She looked up the stairs and steadied herself with a hand on the banister. He heard her cough and then heard her call for their son. The splashing stopped. She looked back, quickened a smile and dropped her eyes, then looked back up the stairs, tapping her fingers on the blue wooden banister, railed with white bars carved into a Victorian style. She ran up lightly, muffled voices echoed down, and then there was pattering. A blonde boy almost four feet tall, round and sturdy, descended the stairs and turned his blue eyes toward Alec. He knelt, and the last three steps went untouched by the bare feet of the boy. He landed hard and thrust out his hands and wrapped his arms around Alec's neck. Alec squeezed his eyes shut, stood and hoisted the boy with him. He couldn't open his eyes for fear this was a dream. When he did force them open he saw Lisa smiling; a two-foot tall blonde girl with bright eyes smiled and sat in Lisa's arms, watching, her round face beaming. Alec saw his brother in the little girl's face, pale and lean, and could almost see Cory hovering over them. Unable to blink or break his gaze, he barely heard Lisa ask how his drive went.

"Fine," he told her.

"I want to show you something, Daddy," and Billy jumped to the floor, grabbed Alec's hand and led him on. The entry hall ended in a T in front of the stairs, and to the right headed straight toward a bedroom. They passed a closed door on the left that gave to a full bath. Across from it was a large archway and the den, complete with a big screen TV. Down from the bath was another archway that led into the library and a glass-enclosed porch. They walked onto the porch now littered with kids' toys, and a bike with training wheels. Alec smiled. He could remember when this whole room was a bedroom, along the wall opposite the archway was once a California-king size bed. Billy straddled the bike, honked the horn.

"Mommy said we could take the wheels off in a few more weeks when I get better."

Alec smiled and looked at his wife. Lisa looked at the floor, then woofed as the little girl jumped out of her arms, screaming at Billy that it was her turn to ride the bike. She tugged at his shoulder, her tone incessant, and then she looked back at Alec.

"Uncle Alec. It's my turn."

"No Kimber," Billy yelled back. Then he looked at Alec. "Daddy. Tell her its mine."

Lisa walked over and hoisted Kimber into her arms, the little girl's face reddening. "Tomorrow, sweetie. You can take turns tomorrow." Kimber jumped to the floor again and started to walk away, arms folded across her chest, chin down. Alec squatted, watched her then called Kimber by name.

"Come give your Uncle Alec a hug."

"She doesn't have to," Lisa said, then looked to Alec. "We've got to go to bed."

Kimber ran over and hugged her uncle, offering a smile before remembering she was mad, and started to walk away again in the same manner as before. Billy leaned on his father as Lisa led Kimber into the bedroom, neither looking back.

Alec stood and swooned. Lisa returned and said it was time for Billy to go to bed and their son jumped from his arms. Alec excused himself to go get unpacked. He asked if the kids were in the next room and Lisa said they were. He grabbed his bags from the entryway, stopping to look back down the hall. The light in the den was low, a cartoon on the big screen. The door at the end of the hall was ajar, and Alec could see Lisa kneeling over a trundle bed, pulling covers up. He took a riser, glanced back at the grandfather clock and sighed. Then he mounted the stairs. At the top the stairs turned ninety degrees, and after two more risers he opened a door to an L-shaped hall that bent to the front of the house. Behind the door was another, leading to the rear of the house, half the room still attic space and the other half a modified bedroom. The apex of the roof joined here, slanted down either side. To the right of the L was a bathroom with shower only, and ahead it opened to a bedroom. He saw the door leading to the front balcony. To the left was a TV and VCR. Along the right wall was a sewing desk, and along the left was a full-sized bed, turned down. As with every other room in the house, the pastel décor flowed with a continuity that spoke of his mother.

He unpacked slowly, trying to take it all again, most of it passing over him. It wasn't until he heard muffled voices, echoing through the vents too close to midnight, that he moved from the room and crept down the stairs. He crouched at the start of the banister, ear pressed against the wall. Only whispers, voices faint, and he couldn't make out what was said. He thought he heard his name a few times, but it only chilled him, and whatever else he heard faded in and out. He told himself this had something to do with his being gone, but that didn't quell his spirits. So he returned to his room. He closed the door and leaned against it, shutting his eyes, hurt not just from what he heard, but because he had done the wrong thing. Just like when he found Karl in her living room, seven years ago, and just like two years ago. He went to bed but couldn't sleep, just staring up at the ceiling, listening to the sounds of the old house settle.

Faintly he heard a voice accompany him, from either the darkness of the house or the darkness of his mind. An old cracked voice that, for all the fear it instilled, was only trying to comfort him. It sang a child's song—he felt as though he were being rocked—and called to him as he waited for the dawn to come.

TWO
Cory

Billy was ready for bed when his mother tucked him in. He closed his eyes and rolled over on his side, tucked his legs up toward his chest and pulled his arms in tight under the covers. His daddy was home. He smiled. In the darkness—it wasn't completely dark, thanks to the light in the closet—his eyes wandered; they wouldn't stay shut. He didn't understand that. He was tired and he should be going to sleep, but he couldn't. His eyes kept dancing across the room, watching the shadows. He looked and noticed Kimber wasn't asleep. She lay on her back, staring up at the ceiling, her hands folded across her chest. She was awake too, and if she hadn't been he wouldn't have felt the need to talk. But she was awake so it was okay; she wasn't even yawning.

"My daddy's home," he said, obviously pride in his voice.

He smiled. He knew his mom and dad were mad at each other, and his dad left. He didn't know all about why, that's something they didn't talk about with him in great detail. He didn't like it. He missed his dad, and didn't like seeing him only when he came to town. Any time Alec came to town to spend time with him it only made Billy sad. But all that was over now, because Alec was home, and something told Billy all was going to be okay.

"I know," Kimber answered him. She didn't sound as happy. Billy leaned up on his elbow, watched her, a little scared because she wasn't moving or blinking. He asked her what was wrong.

"I saw my daddy last night," she said. "I told him I missed him but he said he couldn't come home." Billy furrowed his brow. Her daddy had been gone a while, and he was in Heaven, as his mom and dad had told him. Kimber's dad and mom were in Heaven, and that's why she had to live with them. What he didn't understand was how she could see him, unless he was a ghost. He pressed his lips together until they whitened and stared at her. He shivered; a ghost had been in there room. He knew what that was. He had overheard his mom and dad talking about them, and had seen something about them on TV, and Robbie at school told him about his grandmother being a ghost and turning on lights and moaning and wearing a sheet and banging things around and moving things. Ghosts were what was left of people who died. They shouldn't be here; they should be in Heaven. He had no concept of good ghosts verses bad—not at five, anyway—he just knew they should not be. The very thought scared him.

She tried to talk to him some more but he didn't respond. Too shaken now, he rolled away from her and curled back up under the covers. He tried not to think about ghosts; he thought about his daddy being home. Finally his eyes grew heavy; he yawned and he felt himself drift off. When the idea of ghosts forced itself back in he was all ready to dream, and it didn't bother him that bad. He dreamed, and didn't remember when he woke the next morning what the dreams were, but he was sure it wasn't ghosts.

Cory felt the tension as Alec had walked through the door, and now he paced the attic. What once had been solely attic space—closed off by a door from the rest of the upstairs—had been converted by their father to a makeshift bedroom. Cory spent most of his time here. Half the room had been finished with boards, carpeted, a space dry-walled for a closet where what was left of Cory's clothes hung. He ran his hand along the wallpaper that abruptly ended as the room changed back to attic, with its skeleton support beams exposed and blown insulation filling in between. He felt the plaster of the closet wall, pulled the door open and stared. All his clothes were pressed to either side, except for one pair of jeans and a shirt, hanging on their own hangers, in the middle.

The shirt was torn, stained purple and stiff after drying on the hanger. The jeans were in similar shape. He reached to them but didn't touch. He couldn't touch, because if he did he would remember the accident. That was the only night he didn't want to remember. Justine's passing couldn't be staved by machines.

He shook it off, lowered his hand and turned to the attic. He walked along a single beam, hands in pockets, head lowered, contemplating many facts he wished he didn't have access to. He stepped across a bed of insulation to the next beam, paced toward the makeshift bedroom, and before his feet touched the carpet he turned along the next beam and walked back. He continued that way, traversing the room back and forth, one beam at a time, hands never leaving his jeans, eyes never raised to watch where he was going. He paced until he reached the outside wall, and the ceiling slumped to lower than his shoulders. Then he turned and walked the same way, till he reached the other side of the room. The tension had been thick, when Alec came home.

Lisa wasn't inviting, and Cory saw that had upset Alec. It would be hard for them to rebuild a relationship with Lisa still angry with him. And whether or not Alec wanted to put the rest of them at ease and end this haunting life, that wasn't entirely his decision. There was more, Cory realized, and he reached the other side of the room, turned and began to tread back.

Alec was scared. He was going to need the disenchanted spirits of the Bradshaw family home. Exercising them now would not be an option. Because despite all their best efforts, soon Karl would walk back into their lives, and bring something he, Alec, Lisa, even Cory and Justine—all of them—had awakened seven years ago. And for the sake of the children, for Alec's son and Cory's beautiful little girl, none of them could leave just yet. Cory wondered if Alec realized all this, or if his fear was something irrational, formed deep down that couldn't yet be vocalized. Whatever the case, Alec was afraid. Cory looked up, and found himself in the basement.

His back was to the garage door; on his right was his father's old studio. His father sat at the desk chair, oblivious to everything but what was on the monitor. Two computers were on the wide desk in front of him, and to his right and just behind was a mixing board and a reel-to-reel. He had a DVD recorder, a CD writer, and in the adjacent room microphones and speakers spaced around. The vocal mike was pushed against the wall in the main part of the basement, out of the way of Lisa's car. Just in front of the mike sat a Leslie, and an old heater never used anymore, its wires stiff and crusted from lack of movement. Cory walked around Lisa's car, hands still jutted into his pockets, frowning, surveying the dead studio. A monitor clicked on, and Cory wondered if this was his father's heaven. He had lost any idea of what this place meant to him, without Kimber and Justine.

He walked upstairs, through the kitchen, into the living room. Darkness seemed so natural; the house seemed more peaceful at night. He traced his fingers along the hummels over the mantle of the fireplace, and outside he could hear the mockingbird sing. It had been his grandmother's bird, always coming around so she could feed it. She died eight months ago, the last of them to go. Alec had received the call; he and Lisa had just returned to the house, and he was slipping fast. Cory watched him that night take the call, turn and recoil from whatever he saw on the couch. He must have seen her, how she looked as she transitioned to death. He turned his back on the hummels and walked into the entryway.

For their fortieth anniversary, Grandfather Bradshaw had given Grandmother Bradshaw—and Cory snickered at the gift—a grandfather clock. For the past eighteen years it had been frozen at 2:15. Alec had found their grandfather, the day the clock stopped, in the early afternoon; he was the first person to race into the house. When they called Albert's wife she rushed home from her vacation with Will's sister, and the clock hadn't worked since. Why keep such trinkets? Cory wondered, shaking his head at the clock. All these things can remind us of are the things we want to forget, like the clothes in the closet.

He walked back into the living room and felt the tap on his shoulder, as he began to wonder about his wife and mother. Neither were subtle, neither left behind such simple reminders as a few objects. He could see her in shadows, watching him, and lowered his eyes. His mother wouldn't move into the light of the moon; she hadn't since the night her own heart gave out at the loss of her husband.

"You didn't seem to mind the fact that you left two sons and a grandchild, when your heart broke."

"That's not fair," she whispered. "You were both adults. You were both married."

He shook his lowered head. "I just want to hold Kimber again. Just once. I've tried to be there for her. And Billy. I've tried to help Lisa."

"You can't be there for Kimber."

He nodded, and still his face grew red. His lip quivered and he started to slap the wall but withdrew his hand before impact. "My brother's an asshole. I've been there. We all know it."

She reminded him again how he could never really be there. He began to pace, wishing she'd fade back into the shadows, wondering why she couldn't just leave. And deep down he knew what she was getting at; there was only one way he could be there for any of them now. He had to be the one to warn them. Cory had to be the one to show Alec what he can't know he's already afraid of—the shadowfolk are coming.

"Why can't any of you show them?" he asked.

"Because we have to save our strength," she answered, and then the shadows enveloped her, and Cory was left alone. He leaned on the wall, sighing, eyes closed, listening to the silent house. He swallowed hard and felt himself trembling. He couldn't stop, so he stayed in the entryway until the dawn, a part of him wishing Alec could truly put all the ghosts to rest. Another part of him listened for the sleeping girl he once held, as he came to the realization that he would never again be able to ease Kimber's disquiet.

THREE

Lisa

Lisa poured a cup of coffee in the dark kitchen, her vision hazy, her mind slow so that she caught herself staring several times out the kitchen window. The blackness outside highlighted in pre-dawn blue, shapes vague and just taking form and substance, hypnotized her gaze and trapped her attention in the early recesses of the late night shadows. She had beaten the sun to rise, as she often did, and realized she did it more now that Alec was home. There was too much on her mind to sleep, nowadays. There were too many questions, such as: Just how mad at Alec was she? And while such plagues robbed her of sleep, her mind couldn't function enough to answer them rationally. Any movement out of place could startle her, and did, as she realized she wasn't alone in the kitchen.

"It's too early in the morning," she began, facing the counter and unable to turn. But a whisper came, like a calm wave lapping at the shore, cold and forcing a shiver to her flesh. Then it was all gone. Regaining her nerves, she removed her hands from under her arms and lifted her cup of coffee. The trembling had subsided enough that the coffee didn't threaten to spill, as she walked into the living room and sat upon the loveseat, placing her cup on the coaster on the nearby end table. She blinked, stared at the coffee table, took a deep breath and blinked again. She lifted the coffee and slurped it, swallowed it like an acidic headache pill and sighed, blinked, and stared.

That dick, she thought, and her brow began to furrow. She picked up the coffee and gulped another mouthful and blinked three times. To think he can just come back, and she thought of the sound of his voice as he spoke. That pathetic softness—he was soft during college, she remembered—and it was more than just the words he used, it was the tone, the intonation, the way he paused his sentences and formed his lips and his body language and he thinks he can just walk back in here and what?

She felt like screaming out. She finished her coffee, nearly slammed it too hard on the coaster, and looked around. Her face began to flush, and grew redder as a steady thump reverberated from the stairs. She didn't have to raise her eyes, didn't want to raise her eyes as she listened. It was too early in the morning to see him, as her tired mind reminded her of the scenes of his descent into mourning, away from her and away from the kids. She could see him packing his suitcase, unable to communicate anything to her. He had showered while she got the kids ready, and had left after she returned from taking them to daycare. He had waited for her to return, so he could say nothing to her. So she could stand there and watch him and try to find something to say and he could have the satisfaction of walking away without giving her a cursory glance, and without granting her a single word. He had acted like a child, then, and she raised her eyes. He carried two spiral notebooks down with him—in one of the spirals there was a pen—and she saw his morning face, just touched by dawn and receding shadows. He was acting like a child still, she realized.

He gave her a nod and turned to the kitchen, returning with both notebooks under one arm, and a cup in his other hand. *Milk and two spoons of sugar*, she thought, and he mistook the move of her lips as a smile. He sat in the recliner adjacent to the other end of the loveseat, took a sip before setting the cup down on the glass-top coffee table. She huffed as he leaned back, pulled a coaster and slapped the cup down on it.

"You'll leave a ring," she said, stood, carried her own cup into the kitchen and refilled it. But she wanted to be different from her first cup, so she included a third spoon of sugar, and added enough milk to make hers a little lighter than his. She didn't think to question why she walked back into the living room and sat down. She didn't really want to know what was in the notebooks, though she asked.

"Experiences—about what I've done the last six months. I think I have just enough for a book."

"Takes two notebooks?" and she took a sip of coffee.

He sighed. "The other is for a fictional book about my family. Call it solace, or cathartic, or whatever, seal the chapter on my mourning for them."

She took another sip of coffee, and decided to survey the room to see how different it looked in this early morning light. She heard him say something and she looked up, raising her eyebrows as though she didn't hear him.

"I'm sorry for running away," he said again, lowered his own eyes and pulled the coffee to his lips.

She stood and picked up her cup. "You were hurting," she said, and walked into the library.

He didn't follow; she was alone.

She stared at the row of bookshelves, the line of leather bindings and spines with fabric headers, gilded edges, the antiquated volumes of texts separated from newer editions of hardbacks, with their dust-jackets and heavy paper and colored headers around their glued binding. His father had been such an avid collector, coming from a home life where Alec's grandfather saw uselessness in books. The fiction was segregated into genres and the general "literary" fiction was alphabetized. The nonfiction was categorized as well, art and photography and poetry and all things related distinguished from the sciences, from books on religion and philosophy. History and biographies were sandwiched between regional studies and Americana and medicine and law and political science neighbored their corresponding fields of general studies; next to philosophy were books on the occult, just between myths and then started the religion. Lisa felt herself dizzying.

She took a sip of coffee, perusing titles, understood now why Alec had returned, and why Cory refused to leave. As Alec ran, Cory had stayed. Cory had also been the one to tell her the truth, seven years ago, when Alec left the first time and for a second, she briefly entertained being with someone else. For all his abruptness and brashness and for the number of times that—despite his good intentions—he had crossed the lines, Cory had his honesty. That he could summon such a thing when he had to, when it was needed, was commendable. It wasn't that Alec was a liar—he was quite honest, in his own right—but Cory had used that honesty to bring her back to Alec once. Now, before matters could be resolved with her husband, she needed to find such truth within herself to do what might not be capable from the Great Ghosthunter: she would have to quiet this house of disenchanted spirits, starting with Alec's brother.

Alec felt paralyzed. He helped Lisa get the kids ready in silence, but he could barely acknowledge anyone. He watched them pull away in the car and it wasn't till they were gone that he mounted the stairs to his bedroom and opened his suitcase. He hovered over it, staring at how easy it would be to leave again. He could pack and drive off before she even reached the city limits. He could be gone, and they could get back to being happy.

No, something said, and for a second he thought he heard his mother. More than that, he thought he could feel her—he thought he could feel all of them—and he shivered. He repeated what he heard them chanting.

"If I leave it will be too late. It's almost already too late."

He dropped his suitcase on the floor and pushed it under the bed.

He never let on that he had thought about leaving, after she returned. They didn't talk much. After the kids came back from school he played with them, or watched while Lisa played, and still kept his secret, hoping the ghosts wouldn't expose him. He felt the hours tick by; the afternoon dwindled into twilight, and soon it was dark outside. Lisa cooked dinner and offered him some, which he refused, watching them eat, trying to help her clean the plates and put them in the dishwasher but she had a system down that left no room for a second person, and no chance for him to break in. When done she clapped her hands together and ushered the children into the bathroom.

He offered help, as clothes flew off by her nimble hands, and the naked kids jumped into the warm bath together. She ignored him, for the most part.

"They always bathe together?" he asked over her shoulder, his voice muffled so only she could hear.

"No. I'm just tired tonight."

He nodded, asked if there were anything he could do and she said no. Then he turned and walked upstairs.

Alec turned his computer on and pulled up the first screen. He had spent most of the day transcribing hand written notes to the computer's hard drive, and read what he had. He turned the notes on screen into a brief outline, using a large font, the TAB key a lot, the CAPS key some, and bold print. He reset everything to normal, and waited till he had typed a paragraph or a point in the narration before deleting the corresponding outline point. He did this, remembering that he heard nothing from Lisa all day and wondered what she had done to pass the time.

His mind began to drift, as he got lost in the narration, as his fingers moved and the only guidance came from the direction the story had decided to take. He closed his eyes, remembering what he saw for the kids the one time he went out. *They'd love it*, he thought, and thought of all the fun they could have, how much use they could get out of them. It would help to unite them, he imagined, and his mind drifted further into outer reaches of imagination, where everything is dark and bleak and nightmares are born. He couldn't pull himself back, and saw himself standing at the door of the kids' room. Night and shadow painted everything except the deepest corners, and there it was black. Sanguine eyes watched the children from the blackness, and he felt the shadows smiling; he saw it lurch forward and the children were still sleeping.

His head jolted up and he blinked, tried to shake it off. But it was still there, pressing on him, and something else. A memory of something yet to happen, something he saw in the eyes of the shadowfolk. He had seen where they came from.

Fingers tapped his shoulder and he jumped and spun. Lisa stood over his shoulder.

"Kids are going to bed. Wondered if you want to say goodnight to them."

He rubbed his eyes and nodded. If last night was any consolation of what was to happen now that he returned, he was to spend many sleepless nights alone. He told her he'd be down in a second, thinking she'd just turn and huff and walk back downstairs. She didn't. She stood there, and he thought he saw softness in her green eyes. He found himself staring at her, she staring back, and wondered what to say next.

"You hurt me," was all he could think of.

"You ran away long before I did," and then she did walk downstairs.

He followed shortly after, his brain jazzed from the episode of writing, worn and reaching for concentration on a thousand ideas, jumbled thoughts making his speech barely tangible as he kissed each child and wished them goodnight. He started to pull the door closed and stopped, staring, a part of him warning that as he closed the door the shadows would come alive. Alec shook off the absurd fear and frowned. Six months was a long time to miss in the lives of a two-year-old and a five-year-old, to leave them without a father. His son, he thought, and folded his arms together. His niece, orphaned, and he thought of the night that drove him over the edge. Lisa was right; he had run first, and that night was what drove him away. Cory's temper, that part of him that made him stubborn and cold and keep pushing when common sense would tell another man to back off, had pushed his argument with Justine to the point of distraction, while they drove home from Alec and Lisa's apartment. That was all Kimber could tell them, and Alec couldn't imagine what had set his brother off. Cory was never violent, never abusive that Alec could remember, but he loved to argue and push his point and get heated. What had Justine said, or what had been said earlier to set Alec's younger brother off in the car, and cause him to miss the oncoming truck with the flashing lights and the sign that read OVERSIZED LOAD, and cause him to miss the semi that followed carrying the double-wide home? What had been said that could cause him to take the turn in the road a little wide, only seeing when it was too late? Alec didn't know, and the thought chilled him now. He looked up and around as he walked into the living room, frowning, shivering. *This house has more ghosts than life,* he thought, and listened to the shadows drift through the night.

FOUR
A Surprise for the Children

The boxes were hard to unload, and Alec was somewhat thankful that Lisa gave an excuse, volunteering her own absence from the house. A dark part of him was jealous, and his mind shifted constantly to thoughts of her and another meeting with the same man—or a different one. How unlike the last time this was, and he feared any chance for reconciliation was impossible. But he worked nonetheless, weighing down the instruction booklet with a couple of bricks, toiling in the front yard under sun. In the distance he heard a clap of thunder, and realized the summer storms were beginning early this year, and earlier in the day. It was going to be hot this season. *Just like the last time*, he thought, and didn't fathom that it was nothing like the last time he left and returned. The last time—seven years ago—there was another man who hoped, but couldn't steer Lisa away. And last time she had welcomed Alec back with open arms. But why remember that, he started to ask himself, until he saw it all unfolded in front of him. Because this is the same story, he realized. What happened then affected now, because then led to one of them being hauled off, after they had awakened the shadowfolk, after he reunited with Lisa, and after Karl met her.

Seven Years Ago:

Alec sits in the middle stool, between his brother and best friend. His best friend Karl has red hair cut short, is tall and lean and just a couple years older than Alec. This is his second try at school, a philosophy major who tries to sound logical. He holds his alcohol better than Alec; Alec can hardly balance on the seat.

Cory notes the dark atmosphere. Alec's younger brother isn't of age but he hasn't been carded yet. He's taking it slower than the others but he's still swaying. He's not as tall as Alec, but they resemble each other in the face—Cory has a hard countenance, as though life has treated him unfairly—and he is lean, like Karl.

The franchise sports bar is dark, with muted TVs hung around the counter, music playing in the background, a large restaurant seating area decorated in green vinyl with cedar frames. Alec sees Justine walk out first, carrying a tray. He points her out and Cory perks up. He stares agape, orders a beer while his eyes follow her to a table in the corner, and watches enthralled as she delivers the food to a family of four.

When Lisa emerges Alec gets lost. No one notices. Karl is focused again on a basketball game, Cory is following Justine as she heads back to the kitchen. Alec shakes them and points her out. "She is cute," *Karl admits, his eyes away from the game a little longer than Alec likes. Alec notices, wonders aloud if he should talk to her, they say no and he suggests they go to another bar. He steals another look at Lisa, catches Karl doing the same, and regrets bringing them along.*

I've only known her five months, *he thinks. And he's sad. He's about to lose her, he knows. Their coffee is spiked and they sit at a table in a coffee bar on Dickson. Students are walking the sidewalk, entering doors and leaving hung on each other's shoulders. There is a concert up the road, and across the street a jazz band is entertaining at the arts center. Karl asks if they want to go shoot some pool and he's loud, looking right at Alec.*

Alec straightens, tries to focus on his friend as Cory shakes his head. Karl stands, says he'll be right back, meets some guy at the door wearing a jacket, walks out with him for a few minutes. When Karl returns he grabs Cory, snags a couple of straws from the bar counter, and the two walk out back. Alec orders another beer.

He's thinking about Lisa. He frowns, says to the people at the next table he wishes he could hold her once. They nod and wrinkle their brows and try to resume their conversation. Karl and Cory are sniffing when they sit back down. Alec watches them, not so drunk as they think, watches them snicker at him.

"I'd be a good boyfriend," he says, downing his beer and waving to the waitress.

Karl throws up his hands in disgust. "Why would you want a girlfriend? What do you need one for?" He holds his hands out, fingers together, thumbs touching, a diamond in the middle. "That's all they're good for. Other than that, screw 'em."

Alec nods, hopes that'll shut Karl up. Karl keeps going and Alec tunes him out. Somehow, and he's not real sure at this stage of inebriation, Lisa is different. She's different than other girls he's met, been friends with. She's different than these two, and he looks to his brother and best friend. She's like me, *he thinks. He stands, says he has to get something to eat, walks out before they can stand to join him. He doesn't want to be around them now, because something else is speaking deep within. It tells him it doesn't matter how different she is, nor how similar she is to him, because he is going to lose her, and never see her again.*

It isn't even a week later when Lisa calls and Alec comes. She lets him in at the door, slips her arms around his waist then pulls back, surprised at the softness. Alec wants to tell her he's sorry. He steps further in and sees Cory, sitting with an arm around Justine. He smiles. Then he sees Karl.

Lisa moves back to a seat by Karl. He's lounging in the seat where, two months ago, Alec sat after smoking with her. His arm is over the back of the couch, and when she sits his hand just touches her shoulder. Everyone looks at Alec.

He can't vocalize, even rationalize, the pain he feels. Any words to describe it would seem trite. He has strength enough to meet their eyes. Lisa starts to tell him to sit down, they've got the greatest idea for today, to celebrate the end of the semester. He cuts her off. He waves them off and says he has to go. Then he leaves. He stays gone for three months.

⁂

He started with the easier of the two pieces. The items pulled from the box were a number of tightly coiled, thick springs, a half-dozen or so U-shaped pieces with the slightest bow in the middle, twice as many straight metal rods with crimped ends, and a large mesh canvas mat about sixteen feet in diameter. He pulled last the curved railing and spent his time sticking two straight ends to each end of the U, putting on the curved frame and then connecting each of those assembled pieces. The tricky part was attaching the black mat in the center to the curved rods by the springs—the first springs were easily installed, but as the mat became taut the last of the springs were more difficult. He stepped back when done, pressed the mat firmly with his hands—it was tight and provide a good bounce—and finally tied the plastic cut into a circle to the legs over the exposed springs. He stepped back and surveyed the trampoline. Lisa will want to get a safety net, if she lets them keep it. He smiled, and unable to stop his memories, let them continue as he opened the next box.

⚜

The first week:

He's drunk again; he can barely stand. He pokes again at the soft doughnut around his middle—it is inconceivable when he wears clothes—and curses himself for allowing her to hug him, arms around his middle rather than around his neck. The phone rings. It has rung many times over the past few days, since he left them all sitting there in her living room without so much as an explanation. The calls are from either Lisa or Cory—this time it's Lisa. He listens on the answering machine; her voice is shaky. He staggers back to his couch and plops down, splashes beer on his shirt and tries to zone it out. When that beer is empty he carefully stacks it on another by the trashcan, his wall is higher than the thirteen gallon flip top behind it. He looks over at the sink full of dirty dishes and flies and gnats buzzing around. He opens the fridge; there is no food but there is a case of cold beer, and a smell. Milk had leaked from its carton, spilled in the fridge and while the carton of milk was gone, the spill hadn't been cleaned.

Sure Karl isn't soft, Alec reasons, popping another can open and falling onto the couch. He isn't hard either. He's lean. If I did all the drugs he does, I'd be lean too. He pokes again at his stomach, holds up his left arm and examines it—thin. He gulps this beer down. He turns on the TV but can understand little, and three beers later he passes out.

The second week:
It's a good thing summer has started, because he would have never made class. He pulls himself up, looks in the mirror at his dark eyes, sagging pale skin and ruddy complexion. He is haunted by Karl's words, spoken the night they and Cory visited Lisa's work, on a bar on Dickson Street later that evening. Those words juxtapose Lisa's own desire, the day she poured her heart out to him on the back stoop of her duplex.

"You don't need a girlfriend, man," Karl had scoffed, his tone belittling. "You just need some pussy every once in a while. That's all it's about."

"I just want a guy to snuggle with every now and then," Lisa had said. "Sometimes that's better than sex. Just sleep together."

He sways. His balance is gone, though he's pretty sure he's sober. He runs his fingers through fine hair, turns on the faucet and splashes water in his face. When he's awake enough he takes a shower. He watches TV, pays no attention to what's on, goes out one time to by another case of beer, early enough so it will be cold by five o'clock.

His fridge must be broken, because at four when he grabs the first one it is barely cold. Finally, when he finishes the case at nine-thirty, the beer seems cold, or maybe he's just too drunk to care. Cory has called, saying Lisa wants Alec to call her. Karl has left one message, speaking as though nothing has happened. That was several days ago.

He wakes at six and begins his routine—standing in front of the mirror, trying to finish sobering up—and he remembers something from the night before. Early in the evening he had emailed Cory about workouts; he had gotten a reply. Among asking him where the hell he was, and why the fuck he wouldn't talk to them, and what his damn problem was, Cory included a workout used by Army Green Berets and Navy SEALs and Marines. Alec deleted the message, but only after pulling the workout to his desktop. He walks to his computer, turns it on, chokes back a dry heave and pulls up the workout.

The eighth week:
He huffs, forces out two more pushups, gets to his knees and takes a drink of water. Sweat rolls off his body, mats his hair and clothes. He turns back to his pull-

up stand and can't believe he's done so many pull-ups. He's never been able to do so many. He blasts through an abdominal routine that leaves his stomach knotted, takes another drink and starts his three-mile run. It is almost seven, and today is his day off, so he'll be able to swim at the lake, too. After the run he showers, dries himself off in the bedroom and looks at his bookcase.

Amidst the books on literature are four books on physics and a couple that are overviews of philosophy. He's done with two of the physics books, but only a third of the way done with the first on philosophy—not even passed Aristotle, to be precise. One book that was his favorite he pulls, flips through and moves the bookmark to the beginning; he'll read it again tonight, try to understand more. It was a book on the origins of the universe, discussed time and quantum theory and written in such away that a laymen like him can grasp it. He can't possibly imagine the math and formulas behind it, but maybe someday he can. Right now he just wants to understand it better, have more than a grasp on it.

He finishes toweling himself off, tosses the towel in his laundry basket, goes to the fridge and fixes himself a couple of sandwiches with sour cream and onion chips.

The tenth week:

They catch him at the lake. He's finishing a mile, 30 laps in the roped off swimming area of freestyle and sidestroke.

He stands, his lean body tan, water running off his shoulders and chest. His head bowed, his eyes closed, he heaves, trying to catch his breath. He hasn't seen them yet. He looks up and all eyes are on him, gaping. He can't help but smile. Lisa returns the smile, and meets him at the water's edge.

"Long time, stranger," she says. She tries to not be so obvious, but he can tell she notices him. She asks him to stay, pats his shoulder, he only shakes his head. He looks and Karl has moved to the back of the group, trying to occupy himself with the radio and blankets and things. He tells them he has to work.

"Bullshit," Cory says. "You're off today. I called." He's bowing up to Alec a little, but not much.

"I've got a second job," he says, and mentions doing some roof work for the bookstore and getting a job re-shingling a guy's house.

"Call sometime," she says, her voice almost as soft as her gaze into his eyes.

The swing set was more complicated, and Lisa returned to see not the completed surprises—as he had hoped—but the trampoline on one side of the yard and a metal frame on the other. Smirking, she stood on the front porch, stood for the longest time with arms across her chest, watching him. He worked without trying to notice her, adding the hooks and assembling the U-bar in between the two swings he hung, the seat of each of those dangling six inches off the dirt. The slide was a pain, with pins inserted that were shielded on all sides by the plastic, and still needed a pin ring to hold them in place, the hoop of which was always larger than the space he had to work with. On the opposite end of the slide he finally pieced together the spinning seat, with the pole from the frame going right through the wheel, and two seats spurring off that would spin on the axis. Next to the slide came the carriage. Most of the seat was pre-assembled, and for Alec it was a matter of securing the rods and seat on the pivot axis high up on the frame. The two-headed horse with bars above either head was simple, and went between the spinning seat and the first swing. He stepped back, surveyed his work, smiled and put his arms on his hips. When he looked back he was surprised to find Lisa grinning, nodding slightly.

"Did you put it together right?" she asked, still grinning, walking up to him and then past into the yard. She put her hands on her hips, walked to the swing set first and tested it: pulled here, tugged there, jostled the chain of the swings and tried to shake the slide. She walked over the trampoline and pushed on it, as though testing the firmness of a mattress, then looked back at him, brow raised.

"Try it out," he answered her.

She shook her head and pointed to him. "You first. You bought it and built it without asking me."

He walked across the yard, kicked his shoes off and rolled onto the trampoline. He stood in the middle, the canvas sagging beneath his weight, looked to the house and began to jump. His knees bent; he jumped higher, and learned quickly how to get more air and soon the lowest slant of the roof fell beneath his height. Another thunder clap in the distance and he saw the cloud circling the lake on its northern shore, away from them, as so many storms were apt to do. He jumped higher and closed his eyes and became vaguely aware of the dull ache in his thighs. Still he jumped.

When her calls brought him down she jumped, shoes off. He saw in her leaps and rolls and tucks the same freedom he had just felt. He was lost in watching her when she stopped and beckoned him.

They tried to make each other fall. They timed their bounces to press off just as the other was landing, and then it happened. Their smiles opened and they were laughing. Lisa nearly lost her footing as she came down and Alec pressed off. She stumbled once, spread her arms for balance and began to squat. As he came down he knew another good pounce would topple her. He readied his stiffening legs as he returned and smiled triumphantly, if not prematurely.

Lisa found her footing and jumped.

His legs wobbled and Alec rolled across the canvas. She was coming down again, laughing, the glint in her eye let him know that she hadn't lost her stance that much to begin with. He made it to his side and propped on his elbow when she came down again and he found himself, rolling again. He was laughing, and for a moment all else was forgotten except that he couldn't stand and she was still bouncing and he was happy. And then it was over.

Lisa climbed down and slipped her shoes on, and left her feet dangling over the side as she tried to catch her breath. He sat beside her, his shoes on, his feet dangling also, staring at the grass and seeing nothing, breathing hard.

"My legs feel like jelly," she said, and he nodded in agreement. She looked at her watch and added that it was time to go get the kids.

He looked at his. It read 3:15. Montessori scheduled its pick-ups for five for when the parents got off work. He told her it wasn't time but she still jumped to the ground and began walking toward the house. He called to her, just her name, and she halted and turned.

"We were having fun."

"I don't feel like having any more fun."

He wondered how hard it was for her to keep from adding the words 'with you,' to the end of that. He added them for her, and her red face burned not with exercise but with anger. She took a hurried step toward him, stopped, stared. Her dark hair strung in front of her face; her green eyes burned.

"It may be easy for you to buy their love," she said, "but I'm different."

"I know you are. I've always known you were different."

"You want to treat me like this, but what you've done to those kids is unacceptable."

"That's why you're angry? I'm angry at myself for that."

"Then we have something in common," she finished, and walked away from him into the house.

His son, his niece, how he could have done all this he wasn't sure, but he sat on the trampoline, remembering all of it and feeling sick. He had left them, and they were too young to understand. They were still too young to understand; too young to be angry when he returned. And now … he looked at the swing set, at the trampoline. Now he was taking advantage of their ignorance, so he could rebuild his family.

"Why not be blunt about it," he said aloud to a bird in a nearby tree. "I'm taking advantage of them so I can get what I want."

∞

It had been a perfect night when Billy was born. He could still remember Lisa, sweating, dressed in a gown, her legs up. Her hand had been slick and through the pain that leapt from her eyes with each contraction, he had seen love. During a break she had looked up at him, their eyes had locked and he saw her soul again. There was a sound—a slap—and he looked over, and saw what her love could produce.

He cut the cord and after they had cleaned the baby off, they handed him over to Alec. He smiled, held tight, brought the gift over and sat by

Lisa. He handed the boy over, stepped back to watch mother and child bond. Both were exhausted, and Billy was ready for sleep, the cries diminishing. Lisa looked ready also. He remembered watching them through the night.

He tried to imagine the spirits of his family watching him through the windows of the home and actually thought he saw them. The panes of glass were fuzzy, distorted by their frost and the trick of the light behind them; he told himself there was no one looking out, because as quickly as he caught sight of them, they were gone. Still, his voice only a whisper just loud enough for ghosts to hear, he asked them all for help. He shouldn't run, he knew, and did this today mean he couldn't get them back? He hung his head, praying for the way things were, not realizing that what he should be asking for was a change for tomorrow.

The last school activity before their parents came to pick them up was recess. For Billy it was a time to play with his friends. Kimber had hers to play with as well, and though they sometimes played together, most of the time they didn't bother each other. Billy walked outside, ready to play with his friends, when he noticed two things. Like most days Kimber's class was already outside. He noticed this, and noticed that where her friends were playing, Kimber wasn't with them. She sat on a swing, her back to everyone, her head hung, her body slumped. Her feet barely moved her on the swing. He approached from behind, could tell she wasn't crying, but something was bothering her, he could see that. He moved to stand beside her and knelt, began playing with the rocks. She took little notice.

"What did you dream last night?" he asked. He didn't want to ask if she saw her daddy again—that idea scared him and he didn't like talking about it. She said she didn't remember, asked him and he said the same thing. He really didn't, but he thought maybe she did and just didn't want to tell him. He wasn't going to push her, though.

They sat like that in silence for a few minutes, disturbed only twice. Once a friend of his came over and asked him to come play, and Billy said he couldn't right now. A teacher came over too, asked if everything was all right, and Billy said yes, they were just talking.

"I don't have a mommy or daddy," Kimber said out of nowhere, when they were alone again.

"Yes you do," Billy said, but he left it at that because he wasn't sure what else to say. Finally he added, "You've got me."

That didn't seem to cheer her up, but she did move. She sank off the swing and crouched beside him, her bare knees digging into the pebbles that covered the ground beneath the swing set. His fingers had been running through the rocks the entire time he knelt there, but now he lifted them. He put his arm around her shoulder and she sat there, against him, allowing his arm. They didn't speak. Recess was almost over, and his mommy would be there soon to pick them up. They stayed like that till she arrived.

Cory braced himself against the window; it was the only way he could stand as he watched Lisa and Alec in the front yard. He felt drained, his whole entity fading to another realm, not strong enough to stay here so he was floating in and out, fading, watching them. He huffed until he remembered there was no need for breath, and so he steadied his chest and stared ahead at the two of them, rebuilding their relationship. *If I should fade out now*, he thought, *would they be okay?* If I quit fighting and let my tiredness win and gave in to it, would they all still be in this house together? If I can't have them, will they have each other?

Maybe not today, he thought, *but soon*. They'll never be back the way they were, but they will be back to the way they were meant to be. And he wouldn't fade away into the shadows. He thought of the grandfather clock in the entryway, of the mantle and its perching figurines, of the bust and portrait in the library and the studio downstairs and all the drapes and furnishings and every nook and cranny of this house. He thought of how easy he could copy all of them, so they could stay their strength, and he would make sure there would be a tomorrow. All he asked for was to not fade, until after the shadowfolk came. Everyone would need his help then.

He watched his brother sit alone and felt Lisa pass by. If what he had planned was as tough as he thought, it would take more strength than he had. But from somewhere he'd get it, he decided, as his clouded eyes showed him an image of his daughter.

FIVE

Justine

Alec smiled and sat across from her. He always woke with wild bed hair, Lisa noticed, as jutting and wild as the Boston Mountains in Northwest Arkansas. She chuckled, looked at his hair and laughed again. To wake with a cup of coffee and this seemed too familiar.

"Why did you come back?" she asked. "Really?"

He frowned, took a sip, tried to meet her eyes but she looked away. "To bury the ghosts," she heard him say. "To put them to rest." She looked at him and found him examining the room, the house, glancing over at the clock. It wasn't till he looked back at her that she re-examined the floor. "See if there's anything to rebuild."

Just don't have him ask me, she thought, because she was considering, and she still didn't know. She had spent all night—to her surprise—considering.

"I need to ask you something."

She waited. She looked up to find him staring at her. She blinked and then remembered to respond. "What?"

"We still have the boat, the Sea Doo?"

As if she could see it here, she nodded toward the fireplace. Outside and beyond the house the road dipped and curved, turned to gravel and wound to the edge of the lake where it touched the water's edge. There was a private dock down there with three stalls, two occupied. She had taken the pontoon out twice this summer with the kids. The Sea Doo ran, and while she liked to whip it around, she hadn't taken it out yet. As good as she was, she didn't trust herself on it with the kids. She told him yes and waited. He seemed to drift, looked as though he were contemplating something, his face pensive under all that bed hair, and despite herself she was bemused.

"Is that what you wanted to ask me."

He looked up, focused his eyes and shook his head, and she realized he was still trying to wake up, which made it all the more amusing. She laughed out, put a hand to her lips and shook her head. He cocked his bed hair and squinted puffy eyes, smiling. He asked her what was so funny. All she could say was you, and while she explained his look, what really lightened her spirits were the memories of so many mornings waking up to him looking like that. The familiarity of times from before, where there was no fighting and there was no resentment, just love and friendship. She realized some things hadn't changed.

The chuckling died down and she made another comment about his hair. He looked up with his eyeballs, wrinkled his brow and ran fingers through it. She asked again what it was he wanted.

"I want to take you and the kids to the lake today."

She looked at him, her mouth open a little, the cup in her hand tilted so that if it held anything, it surely would have spilled. She listened to the sound of a small herd tromping down the hall, bare feet slapping hard wood, and watched as two little ones ran into the living room. Billy climbed into his daddy's lap and Kimber into hers. She met Alec's eyes as she rocked Kimber, saw him rocking Billy also. The eyes of the children vacant and unblinking, the lids nearly joined. There were a few huffs, and whatever energy that had pulled them out of bed waned now, as they rocked. Lisa watched Alec with his son, felt whatever heaviness oppressing her lift, surprised by her own tone, light and hopeful as she spoke.

"You guys want to go to the lake today?" she asked.

They woke up. Billy jumped on the seat cushion; Kimber did the same, added a clap and a squeal.

Everyone got ready to go.

Alec drove the Sea Doo out as Lisa steered the pontoon into the center of the lake. The manmade lake was deep, with bluffs along most of the five-hundred miles of shoreline. Surrounded on all sides by hills covered in green foliage, the lake was for all purposes isolated, the calm of the waves primarily tempered by the amount of traffic on the waterway. Today there was little, and as Alec hit the straight cove, Lisa watched him gun the Polaris 750. *He must be doing near fifty*, she thought, steering and slowing the pontoon as the kids watched him from the railing. He cut the Sea Doo to the right, spinning into a 180, a stream of water walling him out of their vision briefly. She watched to find the Sea Doo still upright, Alec still astride and shaking his head, looking around. Even from this distance she saw him smile, and gun the wave runner again.

The wake of the Sea Doo still rolled over the surface of the water, and Alec caught the dip, gunning it as he exited the trough, the wave runner whining and spinning as it cleared the surface, only air slurping into the intake. He landed and cut another 180, splashing more water, and then he saw it. A ski boat was cutting across the water in the distance. She saw him glance at them, glimpsed another smile. He was off again.

"I wanna ride."

"In a second," she told Billy. Alec hit the wake of the ski boat, caught more air. She couldn't help but smile.

Everyone got their turn—the kids went out with Alec only, and he drove easier with each of them—and after the gas ran down, the Sea Doo was docked with the pontoon. A brief reprise allowed them to rest in the sun, then forced them into the lake. Lisa watched Alec, still so cut and fine in his swimsuit. His eyes, she noticed, fell on her a few times. He seemed pleased. She looked at herself in the sun and realized her body hadn't changed all that much in seven years. Her hips were a little wider, her breasts a little fuller. She had kept the fat trimmed off—the only time that was a chore was after her son was born—and she wondered how much longer she had with this body.

Lisa watched him dive perfectly off the front of the boat, and then instruct the kids. They tried, lifejackets encumbering their moves—she made them put the life vests on before they even left the shore, and it wouldn't be till on land again when they would take them off—and Billy got as far as a belly buster. Kimber jumped in feet first, forgot to hold her breath, so came up coughing water with eyes squeezed. Lisa ambled up to the front, watching them swim, watching him try to instruct them on how to do the freestyle. Billy didn't do bad. Kimber lost interest quickly; it was more fun to splash them with water. Lisa laughed as Alec caught a mouthful, coughed, and splashed both children.

"Your mommy used to teach little kids to swim when we were in college," Alec told his son.

"I want to go to college," Kimber piped in, and Billy said he did too, then he looked at Lisa for verification.

She nodded, dove without a splash and sprinted fifty yards from the boat, turned, swam back. The water was cool but nice after the sun; her only question was how it would feel in the wind. She broke the surface, streamed her dark hair off her face, her skin already reddening to a tan. Alec was smiling, and when she wiped the water from her eyes and saw him, she smiled too.

The sun had begun its decent when they returned home. Wispy clouds drifted lazily at high altitudes. The humidity had risen again, making everything sticky, and on the brink of the western horizon Lisa could just make out the evening thunderclouds. She stood at the door of the garage, leaning on the frame. Alec had taken the kids upstairs to try and duplicate his father's famous tuna salad. She was putting up their life jackets. At her feet was a pile of wet swim suits and damp towels, wadded up with soaked rubber lake shoes. The smell of fish and lake-water wafted into her nose, as the breeze picked up. She could admit to herself that the day was fun, and decided where Alec was concerned, the most she could do now was give him a chance, if he was serious.

She lifted the pile into her arms and turned to walk up the stairs. Taking one last look out the garage door, to the serenity, the peacefulness, she glanced upstairs and realized all was silent. Her eyes squinted. She walked into the laundry room and tossed the pile onto the floor in front of the washing machine, turned and stopped. Something drifted through the air. Something familiar caught her attention, but something she hadn't experienced in a year. She shivered, looked around and caught it again. A scent, the only scent, first smelled in her new duplex in college, with her new roommate. Last smelled a year ago, on a night when Cory and Justine and Kimber had visited them in their apartment. A scent that had vanished that night, and now it was back, drifting through the house.

She rounded the corner and didn't find Alec and the kids in the kitchen. Her eyes darted over the kitchen and dining room. The eggs weren't boiling; nothing was laid out. In duplicating his father's recipe Alec duplicated his father's meticulous nature when it came to preparing the ingredients. He laid out the capers, the pickles and onions, the mayonnaise, the seasoning salt, in the order it was to be added to the tuna. He boiled the eggs first, and the last time he made it the kids helped him peel the shells after boiling.

Nothing had been prepared.

She raced into the living room and around the stairs, stopping only at the bathroom door opposite the den. Alec stood in the doorway. She heard the sound of splashing, and peeked over his shoulder to watch the kids in the bath.

"They had fun today," he said, nonchalant, a smile on his lips as he watched them.

"What about the tuna?" she asked, and realized she sounded frantic. *Over what*, she wondered, *a familiar smell?*

"In a minute," he said, obviously ignoring her tone. "I thought they needed a bath first."

She nudged his shoulder and entered under his arm, leaning on the counter. She gave her eyes only to the children. "I'll watch the kids if you want to go fix the dinner," she said, absent, thinking of nothing but how she had jumped at the smell. She didn't notice him lean over until he whispered into her ear.

"You'd hate for me to get too close."

She turned as he rounded the corner, only the sound of his walking away to speak to her now. With a sigh, she lowered her eyes and looked back at the kids. She sighed again, watching them play, arms folded across her chest as she shook her head.

The tuna was good; she didn't try to speak to Alec. They ate in silence and only addressed the kids. When they retired to the den for television, she made sure to sit on the couch after he had plopped on the love seat. The kids meandered from the loveseat to the couch in spurts, trading with each other, always moving, talking to either or both parents, which was the extent of the communication.

A commercial interrupted the program they were watching, inviting them to visit a far away land, as many commercials do during the summer months. This was for a resort cruise line making a trip around the Mediterranean. What surprised her more than Alec speaking up, or even what he said, was the strength in his voice and the feeling that part of his conversation was directed at her.

"I've been there."

Everyone looked at him.

"Where is that, Daddy?"

Alec smiled and ruffled his son's hair. He explained Europe to the best of his ability to the two children. Lisa had never heard of this trip, watched and listened as rapt as the children.

"Your grandpa," he said to the kids—meaning his father—"sent Uncle Cory and me there one summer. We went to Rome and…"

"What's Rome?" Kimber asked.

He looked at Lisa; she shrugged, a grin forming on her face. He was going to have to explain Rome to a two-year-old.

"Rome was a town a real long time ago before I was ever born, and before grandpa was ever born, and before there was an Arkansas or a United States of America…"

"I can say the Pledge of Allegiance," Billy piped in, and Alec nodded, stroking his son's back. Lisa's grin widened.

"I know. Okay so in Rome they wore togas and had guys called…"

"What's togas?" Billy asked.

"They're like big white bed sheets," Lisa chimed in, and smirked at Alec.

"And had guys called gladiators that fought each other and fought lions and tigers and bears…"

"Oh my," Lisa chirped and stifled a laugh. He shot her a look pleading for more help than that, added a smile and turned back to the kids.

"Why'd they fight each other?" Billy asked. "Were some bad guys?"

Alec shrugged, unsure of how to explain the immoral activities of a pagan society two thousand years ago. "It was kind of like football for us today," he said, and then the show returned, and the kids forgot briefly all about Europe. Lisa hadn't, and caught herself stealing glances in his direction, smiling, her thoughts drifting.

In a thirty minute span of time, on that one channel, they had seen commercials for Sandals Resort, a trip to Alaska, their Southern Europe cruise that inspired Alec's reflections, and Australia. Now one came on for Ireland, "The Emerald Isle" it advertised.

"Your mommy is from there," Alec said, and the kids looked at Lisa with awe.

"Not really," she said and shook her head. "My family came from there a long time ago."

"I'd like to see it someday," Alec said. She debated what he must have meant as he continued, almost to himself. "A great big sailing ship," he was saying. "A hundred foot sailboat with a tall mast and the four of us could sail it across the ocean to the Mediterranean Sea and take a train up through France and another across the English Channel and…"

"Why not just sail the Med.," Lisa interrupted. "Then sail the cape around Spain and France and cut up to Ireland."

He was beaming now, his eyes unfocused. "Just the four of us," and he looked to his son, his niece. Kimber got off the floor and crawled into his lap, sitting on his other knee. He put an arm around each of them, shook his head with a scoff. "Pipe dream. As my grandfather used to say, it's like a bird in a tree."

Lisa frowned. "What does that mean?"

Alec just shook his head. "I think he meant, 'A bird in the tree is worth two in the bush,' but he didn't get it right."

"I've got a bird, Daddy."

Alec looked to Kimber, at what she had just said, then looked around. Lisa too glanced. As her eyes returned to the little girl, Lisa found Kimber staring at Alec. She didn't seem phased; she looked back to the television and pointed at something new. Lisa met his eyes and felt the concern.

The next afternoon the kids pulled Alec out the front door. The trampoline and swing set were still new, and still hadn't been broken in enough. Time, Lisa had come to understand, would change all that. In time they would be front yard eyesores the children would outgrow. She knew her son and niece needed stimulation. The yard toys would provide some physical distraction now, but soon the kids would fall back on the old adages of what they had done daily: walks through the wilderness, swimming and playing; these things provided physical exertion and allowed for the expansion of the mind. What stimulation could their intellects have bouncing on a tightly sprung canvas mat, or swinging on a bolted metal rod shaped like a horse? They would still come back to these things, when the cycle had started again, and she understood that all children lived their lives in cycles. The trampoline and swings would get old, and the kids would move on. And it would start to get cold and the season would change and the trampoline would gather leaves and maybe the swing set would begin to rust from a few rains. And the kids would see them, unused, and would remind themselves of the fun, briefly, until they just got old again. Until finally they would be too big to play on the swing set, and too many springs were missing to keep the trampoline safe. And then where would they go, she asked herself, watching them bounce with Alec.

He pretended to fall; the kids toppled on him. There was lots of laughing and crying out. Alec hoisted his son in the air at arm's length, rolled and Billy plopped into the center of the canvas. He bounced, everyone rolled and Kimber fell on Alec's chest. He sat up in pain, but the give of the trampoline was too great and he fell back, his arms and legs spread, and both kids found the roll needed to stand and tackle him again.

Maybe she still knew her mommy, Lisa thought as she leaned on the stone wall of the porch, *maybe she still saw Justine*. She shook her head and remembered the girl in college, the "first natural blonde," she had ever met. They had roomed together, dated together, and she remembered discussing Alec with Justine on many occasions. First after Justine met him, the day Alec came over and smoked with Lisa on the back porch; Justine had thought he was cute. Then she met his brother Cory. It took both of them to ease Lisa, when all that blew up with Karl. And that night at the house, when Alec was back and everything seemed fine and they were on an adventure, it was Justine by her side when all she had known as reality fell away, and she met something worse than spirits of the deceased; she met the shadowfolk.

She looked up and found all three of them staring at her. Unconscious of her actions, she wiped her nose and without thinking, she smiled at them. They all stared at her, as though she had been ignoring them. If she had it wasn't intentional, and in truth her son had just asked her a question, which, lost in her own memories, she had missed. She took a few steps into the yard and shook her head.

"I told you to come join us, Mom," Billy said, and she thought he was too young to sound exasperated with someone. She looked to his expectant eyes, and to the expectant eyes of her niece, and imagined the four of them frolicking through the yard, bouncing through the air. Then she looked to the expectant eyes of her estranged husband, and then she looked at the yard. Things had been changing in her, and without intent to punish the children, they were things she wasn't ready to face yet. Alec's return and his idea for a reunion, and neither was she ready to face the ghosts. It couldn't be healthy for the kids, for Kimber, every time Cory showed up. But unlike others she had heard about—ghosts trapped in space and time and unaware of their effect on the living—Cory seemed conscious of the world and able to interact with it. She would have to talk to him then, for Kimber and all of them standing in the yard as dusk came on and shadows grew long and stringy across the landscape. The day had been humid, and now the heat climaxed with another storm bellowing its thunderous tones across the hills. The lake pushed most clouds away, except for the most severe. This one didn't obstruct the sun yet, but it sounded directly overhead. The lake may not be able to deter it. As she listened to another roll she realized she'd have to help Cory to understand, before she could do anything with Alec.

"Mom!" Billy cried, growing more perturbed—something else a five-year-old shouldn't feel—and she looked up at each of them.

"You guys finish up," she said, and tried to sound cheerful. She told them she was going to cook dinner, and silently asked for help with both brothers. Most of all, she wished she could feel again, as she had once, and she turned away from them and walked into the house. The smell of lilac and a touch of vanilla filled her nose, such proportions she hadn't inhaled in forever, only their memory a day earlier had sprung them to life again. She thought of Justine how she once was: vibrant, young; Lisa closed the door behind her.

Noises of the children playing in the downstairs woke Alec three mornings later. Dreams of color and detail and imagination and truth left him groggy. The details, and the absurdity of the details that plagued his closed eye, the tricks his mind played to make him think it was real, left him worn. He sat up, listening to the children playing, listening to them bound up the stairs and slide down, the steady THUMP as their butts hit each carpeted riser. He heard Lisa call out to them, "Time to get dressed," and yet they continued, laughing, playing, ignoring her so the next time her voice was louder and then he heard her call for him.

"I could use a little help down here!"

The tone was reminiscent of his mother, and that suggested too frightening a complex for this early in the morning. He blinked and lifted his feet out of bed, felt the carpet under his toes. His mother was a good woman, though, and if Lisa was turning out to be like her it wouldn't be such a bad thought. *As long as she didn't stay on the phone as much as Mom*, he thought as he laughed; he stood and put on his robe, then walked downstairs.

Lisa was dressed in shorts and a t-shirt, plastic thongs on her feet that slapped when she stepped, a comical noise as she chased each child, swatted one and rushed to get their clothes on. Billy laughed, ran forward with his head turned to watch her and lagging behind his butt, running on the tips of his toes. Kimber had been caught, and now her red face was streaked; she sniffled, her arms folded across her chest as she sat at the base of the stairs. Billy ran past her from the den, making a beeline for the living room via the foyer. Lisa followed, slapping, glaring at Alec. Kimber took the chance. She started to stand, to run, not realizing Alec was a riser above her. Actually she realized as she turned, squealed and backed away. Alec had caught her. He hoisted her in the air, and when she saw the game was over she slapped his chest, told him no as forcefully as she could, announced she wasn't getting dressed and she wasn't going to school. He carried her down the hall. Following Alec, Lisa carried Billy on her hip, an arm around his waist, his dead weight somewhere between his fingers dragging the ground and dangling feet. She dropped him on his bed with a huff, stepped back and shut the door as Alec sat Kimber on her bed. He turned and saw her panting, sweating, her face red and he knew by noon she'd be taking aspirin for the muscle strain.

"Next time you take the heavy one, Muscles," she said. They dressed the kids as easily as they had caught them, and by the car ride where both parents rode up front the children had settled.

At school he lifted Billy from his car seat; Billy stopped him before they entered the building. He looked at his father earnestly, no smile on his lips, and asked the question that would haunt Alec for the rest of his life. Worse than a ghost, worse than any shadowfolk, Alec was truly afraid when his son asked what was in his heart.

"How long are you staying, Daddy?"

He kissed his son, hugged him tight, turned and saw Lisa holding Kimber, staring at them. Lisa was the one to answer.

"He's not leaving anymore."

"I had to tell him something," Lisa said when they returned to the car. Alec looked at her, hoping she'd tear her eyes away from the drive in front of them. She only started the car, shifted out of park and they rolled forward in silence.

He stood in the library, the night surrounding him. Every time he thought he was getting somewhere with Lisa, something always set him back. Behind the closed door, the woman to whom he had pledged his life lay without him, and he didn't know from one night till the next if his return was all she hoped for. Deep down, he understood she might not know yet, either.

He turned to walk upstairs by way of the sleeping children and stopped. High-back leather chairs positioned around a coffee table furnished the library, just below the marble bust of his father. He sat in one, staring up at the bust, his eyes skimming over the rows of books on the shelves, all placed carefully. He found one too large to fit standing upright, its spine up and leafed edge bearing its weight. He stood, turned the spine down to bear the weight, returned to his seat. From the children's room he heard a cough, sheets rustling.

"Don't let them sleep alone at night," Karl had warned him once, and Alec cursed himself for disappearing as he had. What had he done so much worse, these past six months, than at the very least, allowed them to sleep alone at night? He frowned, missed the jostle of springs, light feet slapping the floor. He didn't miss the little voice. His ears perked, his head turned toward the door, the angle still leaving him blind. But he could hear. Kimber was talking, muttering.

Alec rose slowly, his hands braced against the arms of the chair, lifting him till he could take a step. He took another, and sure the floor wouldn't creak, he hastened his steps till he was in the hall.

Kimber stood in the middle of the floor, chin up, eyes half closed. She'd listen—Alec heard nothing save the soft summer wind tap the eaves and siding of the home—and then she'd speak. Such a verbal communicator for a toddler, her speech was now unintelligible, and directed to whatever she saw with half-open eyes that stood just behind the partially opened door. Except the last two words he heard Kimber utter he could make out, and as he heard them he went numb. He watched the girl climb back into bed; the door of its own accord began to open. He could hear it touch the rubber stopper on the wall, as he turned away. He began to walk, started to look back as he took several steps down the hall, pausing in front of the den. A part of him wanted to look back, as he heard the door drag over the carpet, the knob turn as it closed gently on the kids.

He reached the stairs, imagined footsteps on the carpeted risers as he began to hurry, all rationality escaping him as the two words resonated in his head. "'Night, Mommy,'" she had said.

He pushed the upstairs door closed and leaned against it, listening for nonexistent footfalls. The house was silent, seemingly impenetrable even to the cicadas outside. He sighed once, realized what had just happened, and began to laugh at himself. What he had been afraid to see as the door had begun to open he wasn't sure, but the idea was laughable, because a little child wasn't afraid. And the ghosts here weren't malevolent; they were family.

You forgot to check the thermostat, something inside reminded him.

He swallowed.

Weren't you going to check on the kids again?

He chuckled to himself, still braced against the door, and told himself they were fine. He covered himself up, waited for sleep and listened as the noises outside broke through and began to comfort him, night sounds of the mockingbird singing its numerous songs, the cicadas chirping, crickets like the sweet voice of an orchestra, strumming their legs like violins. He listened to their symphony until sleep nearly overcame him, until he awoke to the sound of his own door opening.

The lights were off save a reading light on the desk behind his headboard. It was a touch light, set now on its dimmest setting, a shallow gold resonance cast in the smallest of circles, just enveloping his head and upper body, some of the floor, some of the bed, all of the desk. He heard the door open, heard it slide across the carpet and touch the wall. In the recesses of night all the noises echoed, and his initial fear was that it was loud enough to wake the children.

He heard footsteps creak along the hall, looked to his feet and waited. He put his hands behind his head, contemplated taking the remote and turning on the television so as not to hear or see when one of them rounded the corner. There was no time. The next step brought the figure into the room, and another brought Lisa into the light. She wasn't smiling. Her eyes—unblinking—were soft. With a roll of her shoulder, she wasn't dressed; the nightgown fell around her ankles.

In a full-sized bed two adults lay on either side. Alec on his side, wanted to reach over and caress her exposed back. In the golden light he could see every contour of her back, the color tan and not painted by the light but glistening. He wanted to massage his fingers over her skin, to stroke her until the sweat dried. Lying in bed, naked with the woman he had pledged to stay beside until death separated them, and he couldn't just touch her. He couldn't just hold. Something in her eyes still forbade him.

"Why'd you come up?" he asked.

"To see if I can feel again," she answered without pause.

He wanted to ask her if she could, but he didn't. He watched her pull the nightgown off the floor, cover herself up while still under the covers. She stood from the bed, looked to the dark hall and finally back at him. Still she didn't smile.

Her fingers stretched out toward him, and he extended his own hand. Their fingers touched briefly before she walked into the darkness. He heard her move down the stairs, slowly, and many times before she reached the bottom riser he imagined chasing after her, taking her to bed and holding her. He could listen closely and could hear her enter her bedroom—at one point he imagined she had stopped to check on the kids—and he rolled onto his back when he thought he heard her door shut.

"I hope you can feel again," he whispered to the darkness.

SIX
Karl Learns Some Things

At thirty, Karl was exhausted; rest was coming. That was the only thought that kept him going anymore. He had been at the halfway house for almost a year straight; no trips to rehab because they found drugs, no vacations to lockdown where they tried to convince him the shadowfolk were a delusion. A year without setbacks was a long time. Part of it was due to the fact that he had found a way to escape.

They showed him their home, and he found solace there, walking amid the reeds jutting from sand as soft as babies skin, listen to the little plots of ground whisper a cry as his feet came down to step. It was cold there, the air always thick with mist, with grass like infant hair tickling his ankles. He never touched the lake, just watched, faces vacant and staring from their final death, most given up fighting, some thrashing still trying to escape the steadily rising water. Karl knelt many times at the shoreline, his feet burying in the sand, nearly touched it but dare not. He didn't want to be trapped here.

This place, he thought, looking around, *was an unintended hell for the lost and innocent.* The shadowfolk fed off those, and knowing that brought up a question in his mind as to what exactly they were. Could they be classified in terms of modern religion, he supposed they were demons, but the idea didn't sit well with him. They were, he knew, disenchanted. They devoured the helpless after stalking them—be it ghost or child— and came here, excreted their remains here in this world. They were— he realized in moments of clarity—cowardly beings that use what they hunted to shield themselves from the one thing Karl knew could break through the water. He had heard them whisper about the deity they feared, about something strong enough to disrupt this world and free their captives. He looked around and decided that they had no captives here; everything brought here had been wiped from existence. This place, this world where he found serenity just in walking, was a graveyard. A part of him asked why this place hadn't been destroyed yet, by that powerful entity that could disrupt their waters. The answer came disturbingly to him—people like a man he met in the halfway house were allowed to exist, a man who had to register when he moved in, and his picture was posted in the paper though he was reformed. Karl had heard this man in the night, thinking about what horrible things he had done, really heard the man reliving it and getting excited by it. Karl wished if someone like that was allowed to exist, then maybe the shadowfolk could bend the rules for a time, and take him to their world. *Let him go for a swim*, Karl thought with disgust; *let him get trapped in the water*. Karl understood why they could survive, and at times he didn't like it. At others, his own dreams gnawing at him to the point of a violent outburst, he was glad he found them. What scared those who watched him was how quick his temperament could shift from one extreme to another.

He sat on his bed, looked at his watch; the house director would be here just before breakfast. He ignored his peripheral sight—a skill now exceptional—and remembered what was important. All that mattered now was getting out, because it was time. Because they said.

He slipped, saw them, checked his door still closed and looked around. Darkness caught at the wrong angle shimmered and he saw the sanguine eyes. It reminded him of Florida, on a crystalline beach when the sun reflected off the water and danced over the stones on the shallow bed of the ocean—they reflecting off his own sight, danced over the contours of the room.

Because we can't, they said, before he asked, "Why can't you just leave me alone?"

Not until we get what we want.

So he watched, all the while practicing everything the director would see. He couldn't laugh after saying that, but maybe a chuckle after saying this. Don't fidget. Don't sweat. He pushed out wishful fancies for drugs to sedate his distemper. But they supplied the thoughts.

How about some grass to soothe? On the heels of that: ganja, pot, weed … or maybe some crack. If you can't be calm, be hyped. You're getting out. You're getting Lisa. And we get the children.

He tried to will himself to stop sweating, stop shaking. His hands rubbed together, and all around him they danced. The door opened. He looked up.

There stood the director. With gray, thinning hair and a pudgy middle, in a short-sleeve collared shirt and khakis, his spectacles perched on his nose, hands in pockets; he smiled. Karl tried to smile back. He clasped his hands together and forced them between his knees. The director asked if he could come in and Karl said yes. The director sat down in a swivel chair, wheeled it over in front of Karl, just smiling. He asked how Karl was feeling. Everything Karl had practiced was fresh, but he knew he couldn't do it. He huffed, he sagged, lowered his eyes and hung his head. The shaking stopped. The sweat began to dry and cool.

"I'm tired. I didn't sleep well last night."

"You've looked tired recently. Still seeing the shadowfolk."

Karl shook his head, only vaguely aware of the lie. He swallowed hard as the realization hit that he'd never be free of this. They were a symptom of his disease—a type of schizophrenia he couldn't even pronounce—probably enhanced by all the drugs. Someone had told him once that you were clinically insane if you took seven hits of acid in your life.

"I bounce around. Sometimes I think it were better if I was locked up in one place. The way it's been has just wore me down."

The director nodded, reminded him they could only lock up criminals like that. He was just a man with problems, and as hard as this was, it was best. This was his best chance at maintaining hope that he could rejoin society. He asked what Karl thought of the shadowfolk, and Karl chuckled—unrehearsed.

"You said it best. I've got problems. I'm never getting out of here."

He rubbed his hands together, traced his past that led him here, as psychologists were so fond of doing. He found it pointless. "I think some people take comfort in myths and legends, like I do with drugs. It's an escape. It's a chance to avoid reality. It's prettier to think there is some monster under the bed than just life."

"But despite the monsters, and after the drugs have wore off, life is still there."

Karl nodded. If they were swarming he couldn't see. "That's the scariest thing of all." He contemplated everything; like a collage his philosophy, his life the past seven years, was muddled together; as a mobile it hung on a string in front of him, bouncing, twisting and turning. "There are such things as ghosts. Anything that causes us to remember, that won't let the past die. The trick, I think, is to make sure that even if they haunt you, they don't scare you. I've been scared a long time."

"And the shadowfolk?"

Karl shook his head. "I think you're more obsessed with them than I am." He chuckled. He regarded the director a second, felt the gleam in his own eye, kept the smile on his lips. "The future is inevitable, waiting to consume all of us. Unless you're ready to pull the trigger and I'm not."

The director smiled and patted his knee. He stood, stretched with a little pop of his back, offered a hand and Karl shook it. Karl stood and the director spoke, his words inhibited by the smile he wore. "You've come a long way."

Karl stuffed his hands in his pockets, looked at the floor. The smile on his lips was hidden from the director, as the balding man walked away and closed the door behind him. Such a smile would normally be displayed prominently, if Karl weren't afraid that such a triumphant grin would betray him. So he let the man walk away to sign the papers, letting the director think he was humbly waiting, and he smiled.

SEVEN
Alec Makes a Play

Alec pulled the extension ladder from the basement and walked on top of the house while Lisa pruned and weeded. She had told him that with the last rain she found a leak. Alec found rotten tiles, pulled them up, found the termite-ridden boards underneath. He had carried up a skill saw already connected to the plugged in extension cord, and it didn't take him long to remove the board. He sat down, wiping sweat from his forehead, wondering how much of the roof was in this state, and what else was wrong with the house. Below him was Lisa, tanned, firm, bent over the irises, clippers in one gloved hand, weeds in the other. He climbed down the ladder, walked up behind her. She didn't face him when she spoke.

"What were you looking for the other night on the porch?"

He shrugged and said he didn't know. "How long were you on the couch?"

She forgot. She walked into the house, to the kitchen, Alec following. Her hair was pulled up; he could see a drop of sweat on the back of her neck. She fixed two glasses of ice water and sipped hers, leaning on the counter, watching him. They talked about what he needed to do to fix the roof. He said at some point before it got cold the entire roof needed re-shingling. He asked if she had noticed anything else and she said she hadn't, and from there the conversation died. They finished their water, put their glasses in the sink, and he asked if she would go with him to get some things he needed for the roof.

100

"I don't know," she said, lowering her eyes. She mumbled about the gardening emergencies that needed to be done.

He reached out a hand and left it in mid air, saying please. She took it and said okay, let go and they left for town.

They didn't talk that much on their drive, and little afterward. He could feel the tension, in fact, and realized she was going with him more out of obligation than of any real interest to spend time with him. He worked on the roof most of the afternoon, watching her prune the mimosa tree after her weeding was done. It took him that long because of the heat; he had grown unaccustomed to it and stopped often for shade or air conditioning and water. She had entered the house an hour before him, and when he finally came inside he found her in her bedroom, putting the finishing touches on. Her hair was washed and combed, she had applied the only makeup she wore—some eyeliner, lip-gloss, and foundation—and she was dressed in jeans and a nice shirt.

"Can I talk to my wife a minute?" Alec asked.

"What?"

"I think we were both thinking about some things the other night. Maybe even thinking about the same things."

"Possibly." She had turned her attention back to the mirror. The pain in his stomach got worse. Beyond the lean muscle he had acquired, he felt the same inside, and that realization just hit him. He felt like a soft kid still in college, lean but flimsy.

"There's a lot of tension in the house," he said. "Not just since I returned, but there has been for a while. For a couple of years now."

She admitted there had been, still focusing on the mirror.

"I think we have to work through it," he said, "for the kids."

She rested her hands on the dresser, hunkered over, her eyes down and when she raised them she looked tired. "I don't know," she said. And then she straightened and walked by him.

He watched her round the corner from the library to the hall. He had grown, he realized, because there was a time he would have grabbed her, forced the conversation on her. Now he just watched her leave, and a second later he heard her car pull out of the drive.

Lisa had gardened to keep her mind off what she knew had to come, and made sure Alec was still on the roof when she came in to get ready. For Alec to ask her to town as he had, was something she realized she wasn't ready for. The public eye to see them, as though they were back together, when they still had so much to deal with. Old feelings had swelled when he walked through the door, some good, some bad, and she was left confused. When he entered her bedroom and began to talk, she pleaded silently for someone to keep Alec from starting in.

At least he didn't press his point, she thought as she drove to town. She realized he was right. They had things to settle for the sake of the children, if not for each other. She knew it wasn't healthy to harbor the anger for a long time, but it was hard to let go now, after he had been gone so long.

The turn came for the street where the school was located, and she didn't take it. The town wasn't very big, and in thirty minutes she could drive across the business spur of the highway, turn and take the bypass, and drive through town again. But it gave her time to reflect.

Two radio stations provided the best source for rock in the area. Neither was great. She turned off the radio, her mind empty at first, taking everything in, until her subconscious began steering her. She had seen things in the house—a few nights ago something had shaken her awake—and Alec, though he wasn't talking, had seen something. From his glances to the children's room and his uneasiness around Kimber, she supposed it had something to do with Kimber calling him "Daddy" a few nights ago. *Maybe Justine overheard,* Lisa thought, *and wanted to correct the reference.* But none of this scared her as much as it concerned her. The activity always came in spurts, like the kitten that appeared from nowhere just after Alec's mother died. It had been scratching at the front door for God knows how long, when Lisa heard it mewling. A stray, a baby, and it walked into the house like it always belonged, walked straight into the library as though it knew where it was going and stopped just under the bust of Alec's father. About that time, Lisa realized it was best not to watch TV by herself late at night, or go into the studio downstairs. A year ago, just after the accident, when Kimber first moved in with them she spent her nights talking gibberish in her new room to someone not there. Billy had done that too as a toddler, wanting to see his grandpa and saying goodnight to the bust. What unnerved her most about that was the look in her son's eye, as though his affection had been returned. And then there was the afternoon three days after Alec moved out. Lisa had received a phone call.

She shivered; her mind showed her glass exploding, mirrors shattering in unison and a brief replay of that night seven years ago caused her to jerk the car, pull over and stop in the parking lot of a bank. She gripped the wheel, thanked God that Karl was still locked up, trying to ignore the image of the shadowfolk that night, and the sound as they devoured the ghosts and then stared at the four of them. Their lurid eyes roamed over her, Cory, Justine, and Alec and Alec had held her tight. It was the one time with him she didn't feel protected. She was a levelheaded person, she had a scientific mind, but she supposed a part of her always believed in ghosts. Maybe that was what attracted her initially to Alec; his creative mind so attuned to the romantic, and her willingness to embrace such ideas.

She picked up the children and didn't take near as long taking them home. She parked behind the house, in the basement that opened to a family room with no windows—a cave in the hillside under the house—the studio jutting off to one side. She saw Alec wandering through the studio, looking at all the production gear now unable to work with all the dust caked in it. He smiled and ambled up to the car as she shut the engine off, and the kids jumped out and raced to him. He swept Billy into his arms, hugged his son and kissed his cheek; set his son down and did the same with Kimber, who screamed, "Uncle A" and laughed as he stole all her sugars. Lisa turned her eyes to Billy as a smile waned on her lips. Billy was solemn, put his hand on the wood column that braced one of the corners. It was darker down here, but she thought she saw the boy tremble. She walked up behind him and touched his shoulder. He jumped a little but didn't blink. He stared at the studio, unmoving save the trembling, silent except for the heavy sighs.

"Can we go upstairs?"

She glanced back at Alec, the concern in his face set as deep as her own. Without a word he passed her, lifted his son into his arms with a groan as Lisa turned and picked up Kimber. They trudged up the stairs, Alec and Billy leading the way, Lisa watching her son's eyes focused on the studio. As Lisa pulled to door closed behind her, she sat Kimber down and turned the latch to lock.

Whatever feeling that had possessed Billy, faded as the four of them played in the living room. When Alec's grandparents were still alive, the living room was for formal entertaining. The décor was such that the room couldn't be lent to everyday play, and gatherings were, for the most part, held for special occasions or business guests or Christmas mornings. The tree was always against the partition, just behind the loveseat, and the furniture utilized by the adults—the hearth for the children—where everyone had a pile of gifts to open. Throughout the year to find anyone sitting in the living room furniture wasn't forbidden, just unexpected. It was easier to plop down in the den or hunker around the kitchen. Even after Alec's father had the renovations done, the formal library seemed more a gathering spot than the living room.

While she had been gone this afternoon, Alec had scattered toys everywhere. The coffee-table was a formal battleground with plastic green army men ready to attack the plastic tan ones, all strategically placed like she imagined some relief map in the wardroom of the Pentagon where generals planned battle strategy. On the hearth were a few stuffed animals and some larger dolls, and a pile of books that would entertain Kimber more than the dolls ever could. The hummels on the mantle looked down on the toys, seemed to be frowning at the clutter.

Billy made the rules for the army battle, then proceeded to break them. He took his green tank and decimated the ranks of the tan forces—a tan man with a machine gun held in both hands over his head went flying, disappeared somewhere under the couch—and Lisa found herself laughing at how quickly Billy destroyed what it must have taken Alec forty-five minutes to create. Kimber handed Alec a couple of books with the expectation that he was to read to her; he didn't even finish the first when she was ready for the second, and soon she had picked up her own book to read for herself.

How she was elected the clean the mess alone she wondered about, as she listened to Alec give the kids a bath and tuck them in. They had pieced throughout the evening, and she knew well enough that to set them down to an actual dinner would only leave the food uneaten. She didn't feel like wasting food tonight, and didn't feel like forcing the kids to eat when they'd just throw a fit about it. Lisa had other things planned.

Alec had left her in the living room after the kids were in bed, walked into the kitchen as she was unburying the last of the army men and straightening the room. She could hear him, things banging and jostling around, fridge opening and closing several times. She had worked slow while she thought about what she was going to say, and now she sat on the couch, biting a nail, trimming it down, wondering if she could even call Cory to her. But the noises in the kitchen were a constant distraction, and when they had subsided curiosity overwhelmed her, so she walked around the partition and into the breakfast area. She tried to hold down the gasp.

A rose stood as the centerpiece in a narrow glass vase, over a doily that covered the entire wood surface. Two place settings were at either side: the plates holding homemade chicken Parmesan, mixed vegetables glazed in an Alfredo sauce. A basket of sweet rolls placed by the rose and two glasses of red wine separated the two plates, and beside both were clear glass dishes of salad lightly dressed in vinegar and oil. Alec was lighting a candle when she entered, and looked up and smiled at her. She glanced down at her jeans and shirt grungy now and a little sweaty and felt underdressed in her own home for dinner. She looked up, started to say something, forgot what and shook her head.

"When did you…?" and that was all she could get out; she stopped, mouth gaping, staring at the dinner.

"Last night. Spent most of the night working on it. I thought it would be nice, given the other night upstairs. Something to try and help you feel again."

She dropped her eyes, her mind numb, her tongue heavy. She leaned on the wall and sighed, as though all she had left escaped with her breath. When she looked up at him, there was only sadness. He wasn't going to understand.

"I can't tonight."

It was his turn to be shocked.

"I have to talk to Cory."

She could see his wheels spinning, struck dumb by her words. The lack of sleep he must be influenced by, and a long day working on the roof only to have her run out on him this afternoon, and the playing five hours with the kids and finally putting them to bed and rushing to get this ready to surprise her—he crumpled into his seat, sagged down. When he looked at her she could see he didn't understand, and she realized then the inevitable was coming. *We're going to fight, tonight,* and she realized she didn't have the strength. She turned and walked away, and sat in the living room wondering how to put a ghost to rest.

Alec paced his bedroom, thinking, listening as Lisa's voice echoed up through the vent. The kids had been asleep for an hour. He paced, asked himself why he came back. He felt sick again, cold, too many emotions clouded any rational thought. He wanted to rationalize things, think with a clear head. He paced.

Another hour of listening to Lisa talk to air, and Alec found himself devoid of rationality. He wanted a confrontation. He walked downstairs, nearly stomping, slamming the door closed to the second floor as he walked. He stepped around the partition and saw her.

Lisa sat on the couch. She looked up, looked haggard as Alec appeared, and in her eyes he saw he was intruding.

"What are you doing down here?" Lisa asked, her tone sharp.

"This is my damn house," Alec said, looking up to the ceiling. "Leave us alone." He paced; he yelled louder. The kids could be heard stirring, and one was sniffling. Kimber began to bawl as he raced to the stairs. Lisa met him at the foot, grabbed for his arm but he pulled away, glaring at her. He ran upstairs, heard her footfalls, tried to slam the door on her as he walked to his bureau and opened drawers. He pulled his suitcase from under the bed and opened the first dresser drawer.

"What in hell do you think you're doing?"

He huffed, began to shake, then in a whispered tone, "I'll leave, then. I'll sign the papers if that's what you want."

She turned on him. "You left us, Alec. I can't ever forget that."

"I left because you slept around on me."

"One time is not sleeping around," she barked, then turned away. Her head hung. "You left way before that, anyway."

He began pacing; she turned and backed away.

Alec pointed to the stairs. "You'd rather talk to a ghost then have dinner with me?"

"Quit being an ass."

He walked to the wall, more furious, nearly punched it. "Why don't you go find that guy you screwed a couple of years ago? Even better, huh? Maybe he'll put up with all this shit. My family dying, we were burying them one right after another, it felt like."

"But you have a wife and son who aren't dead."

"Why, Lisa, are you doing this?" She didn't answer. He went on. "So what now? Still want me to sign?"

"You'd have never signed the papers," she snapped, turning away from him again.

"Why, Lisa?"

"I'm smothered, Alec. I'm smothered in your life. And all you want to do is run away from it."

"Bullshit," he yelled. "I'm not running now. I'm here. I'm back. I'm not going anywhere." He lifted the unfastened suitcase by the handle and tossed it, spilling clothes everywhere as it crashed with a boom that resonated through the house. "So why the hell are you doing this?"

She dropped her eyes, folded her hands in front of her, mumbled something. He stepped closer, "What?" and stepped closer again.

"Because I still love you," she said, giving him her eyes, virdescent and filled with tears. He stepped back, couldn't look away from her, couldn't unlock their joined gazes. He swallowed hard and kept looking. She still was the girl he met seven years ago, a living paradox: wise yet full of innocence, intelligent yet dreaming of things that bring bliss only to the ignorant, careful guards around her heart, which she'd still give him wholly, without hesitation. "You've loved me since the first day I walked into class," she said. "You just never realized it until later."

"I still do," he said.

"After you left, Karl tried to kiss me one night. It felt wrong. Like I was doing wrong by you." She sniffled. "I knew when you came back around. I saw all you had done to change yourself and I thought *That dumb shit, I loved him just the way he was.* But you went and changed yourself and got all melodramatic with your actions and I knew. I've always known you loved me, Alec Bradshaw. I only did what I did because you were gone, and I was lonely."

"I was thinking it was a vengeance thing. Try and hurt me."

She sniffled again. "Maybe a little of that too. But I was lonely. I needed you."

He fought hard for a deep breath, the anger still hovering in the room, stifling him. "All I want is to take my wife to bed. All I want is to hold you. You wanted that too, once."

He saw her look back to the stairs before her gaze returned to him. "You were about to leave again."

"I won't. You can't let me."

She asked him what they were to do, and he shook his head, said he didn't know.

"The kids are still up."

"I'm sorry." He looked at her, and the past six months swept over him. All the ghosts he had seen, all the phone calls and the conversations with his estranged wife and the few times he saw his son and the uneasiness that came with visitation rights, like he was the outsider; all of it overwhelmed him. And there was more.

The six months prior to that, he saw himself drifting, isolating himself from them, driving her into another man's bed, the not talking, the not holding each other, until he got the word of his grandmother's death and found out about the death of his marriage nearly the same day. He left just after that.

Lisa put her arms around him, caressed his back.

EIGHT
Nature Walk

Alec told Lisa he had to run an errand. It wasn't till he reached he optometrist's office that his fingers touched his eyes and he pulled out the contacts. He tossed them in the trashcan, blinked as his eyes tried to adjust. Everything was just blurred, and he told the clerk he was here for his appointment. On his mind, as he sat and waited, wasn't the fact that even with the contacts his vision had been skewed, suggesting that his eyes were steadily growing worse. Only on his mind was the fight three nights ago. Whether the tension following was solely created by him, or a byproduct of heated emotions, he wasn't sure, but he was ready to diffuse the situation. His best idea involved them as a family, and it would happen after they retrieved the children from school.

His eyes were checked, and his mind jumped from topic to topic. He needed to find a steady job, if he were going to stay. There wouldn't be enough ghosts in Rapps Barron, Arkansas, to provide any type of living. Maybe he could get back on at the school—he'd try but he wasn't sure. There was the local college, as an option for teaching, but they would at least want a master's degree. He could get one from there, but wondered then if the family could afford that. His mind lingered then at that point, making several mental notes that he had to check out the exact state of his and Lisa's finances. If she was ready for that, something else—perhaps the interior devil's advocate that spoke against his rationality—interjected. He thought again of his idea to help smooth things. It was simple, and it provided what they needed most now: a chance to grow together again.

"You want contacts again," the doctor said, snapping Alec back to where he was. He began to discuss the option, the waiting.

"No," Alec spoke up, stopping the man cold. "Just some glasses."

The doctor nodded. They had a wide selection of frames, and his astigmatism should be in stock in the lens; give them about an hour. He called Lisa to let her know that he was on his way home, she said all right and said she was going to get the kids. Her voice seemed warmer, somehow, and he sighed as he hung up the phone.

When he tried on the glasses, he saw better than he had in years.

Alec had just run in to grab a couple more drinks for the kids when he took notice again of the grandfather clock in the entryway. Lisa and the kids were outside, waiting, and in truth his notice was just a glance. But in that glance was just another reminder of how many things had gone wrong. The day Albert Bradshaw died was the last day it worked. Now its hands were frozen on 2:15, the time a ten-year-old boy had walked through the front door in a race with his eight-year-old brother, and found Albert on the couch, cold, unmoving.

He glanced at his watch and saw it was one o'clock, walked out the door and pulled it shut behind him. He tested it to make sure the lock held, then led them toward the wilderness.

Trails had been cut through the forest where kids and parents hiked; today Alec knelt with an arm around each child to point out deer tracks or show them a squirrel or rabbit. Lisa smiled as she watched Alec with them, between her quick glances over the terrain for things that were crawling or slithering too close. Kimber was tired before they were to the halfway point, and after some convincing, Alec lifted her onto his shoulders, her legs around his neck, laughing. They walked fifty feet and Billy began to complain that his own legs were getting sore. His eyes green as he looked up at Kimber, he turned a pitiful gaze to his mother.

"Oh no, big boy. This was your idea. I can't carry you." She looked at Alec. "I about gave myself a hernia lifting him the other morning."

Alec smiled but didn't respond. They continued walking and Billy began to whine.

"Mommy, I'm tired!"

Lisa shook her head. "Sorry."

"I have a solution," Alec said, and he sat Kimber down. She looked at him as though she had just been scolded, folded her arms across her chest and began to cry. Alec huffed. With chin to his chest he watched both kids. Lisa put her hands on her hips and looked at him for an answer.

Alec found it.

A terrapin crawled a quick pace across the trail. Everyone but Alec had their back to it. He walked past all of them, knelt, picked the turtle up by the shell. Its feet and head drew in; Alec held it up and the kids stopped whining, ran up to see the creature.

After letting them touch the shell in awe—Billy asked if it were a snapper before he touched it and Alec reassured him it wasn't—he handed the turtle to his son. The weight caused the boy's arm to fall, but he held on. Kimber immediately wanted it and when Billy handed it to her, she dropped it. Billy scolded her then and picked up the animal, and to Alec's surprise the turtle reared its head and feet, craned its neck and then swung its legs in the air. It made a little gasping sound. Billy carried it for about ten feet, before he decided his daddy needed to hold it. That was as the turtle began to pee.

"Can we keep him, Dad?"

Alec knelt, held the turtle out; it was still peeing. "I thought we'd get some of Mommy's fingernail polish and paint our zip-code on it, and let him go."

"Why?" Billy asked.

"Well, imagine how far he'd get, and the next person who found him would see how far he traveled."

"Cool, Dad."

"If you cover their shell, it'll K-I-L-L them," Lisa said.

Alec looked at her. "No it won't. And we're not covering the whole shell, just a part. Isn't it if you leave them on their backs?"

She shrugged and wiped sweat from her brow. "Getting hot, hon." And all they thought to bring for the kids had been drunk already.

He looked at his watch and agreed. They walked on, neither child complaining about the heat or sore feet because both were too excited about the find. Lisa sidled up to him long enough to whisper "Nice save," and beamed a smile at him. He looked at her, she was a little pale and sweating a lot, and his new mission was getting her and the kids home, getting some water into them.

They returned and Alec told them to enter the front while he walked around to the basement. There he entered the side door, raised the garage door for natural light, and put the turtle in a discarded cardboard box that was cobwebbed and laying under the stairs. He heard them walk down; Billy carried some red fingernail polish and held Kimber's hand and Lisa balanced three glasses of water in her hands. At the bottom of the stairs she handed one each to the kids. His wife and kids hovered over him, blocking the sunlight as he painted the numbers on the turtle's back. When done he recapped the bottle and handed it to his wife. As she took it her other hand jutted, sloshing water and melting ice. She offered a smile. He frowned.

"You look hot," she said, and nudged her hand more. He thanked her, took the glass and took a sip, then handed it back to her. He asked Kimber if she'd like to let the turtle go. She shook her head and folded her hands up under her armpits. He asked his son. Billy yelped. He carried the turtle to the edge of the hillside and set it in the tall grass. Kimber was right beside him. Alec and Lisa ambled up, watching, Lisa was smiling and behind Alec's smile was the thought that he needed to drag either the weed-eater or the sling-blade—or both—out. He shut and locked the side door after they finished. They mounted the stairs first and before he followed he looked out the opened garage door, his finger hovering over the button. The lake was blue, the hills around it green, the sky clear. He pushed the button and watched the scene fall to the light colored metal, the garage growing dark.

It was just a simple glance he took, after the kids went to bed, and it stopped Alec cold. He backed away, unaware of Lisa as she rounded the corner, noticed him, approached and froze herself. They stood side by side, watching and listening. The weights in the back drove the pendulum, a tick at one second keeping the beat. The minute hand moved slightly, and Alec raised his watch for both of them to see. He compared the hands and found that more frightening than anything else.

It was keeping correct time.

"Why is it doing that?" she asked in a shaky whisper. He didn't know why, and all he could do was shake his head. But something whispered to him, reminded him of a warning from someone once a friend who now wrestled with his own sanity. The warning had come during a brief interlude of clarity, and now it made Alec turn, without speaking, walk down the hall and push the door open to the kids' room.

The trundle beds were against either wall. Dirty clothes were piled in between them. Billy lay on his side, curled into the fetal position, buried under the covers. Alec didn't like his son lying like that. Kimber was on her stomach, her head turned to the side, mouth agape, the covers to her shoulders. Alec watched them, remembering the day he came over and found his grandfather. His grandmother withered up after that, and had to go to a nursing home. He remembered that he didn't want to move into the house, when his father had told them of his plans. He recalled how he felt, especially the first few nights here, a feeling of not being alone when you were the only one around, of not being the only one awake when everyone else was asleep. He took cautious glances at every shadow, that first week, and wouldn't go upstairs alone.

His kids lost till the morning, he stood there, and found himself glancing at all the shadows in their room. What if Karl got out, he asked himself, and recalled that Christmas when Albert had told him and Cory about the legend of the shadowfolk. The walk had been tiring, but now he felt a necessity binding that fatigue. He leaned on the doorframe, and watched them till the earliest recesses of dawn.

Lisa watched him from the base of the stairs. He was just standing there, and the same things were running through her mind that plagued his. She knew why the clock was keeping time again. She knew why he stood vigil now, at their door, and that he wouldn't move for the rest of the night. And unlike Alec, who saw the argument as birthing another hurdle in their relationship, she wanted to talk to him now. She had opened up things that she was afraid to open, that she had been holding back for nearly a year, and now she wanted to keep opening them. She could tell he was afraid, but with the grandfather clock running again, she saw the importance of settling this. Time was being kept for all of them now, and if Alec's fears won and nothing was settled, then everything would be lost. Just don't let him run again, she found herself praying.

Seven years ago:

It is overcast; a week has passed since Alec last crossed her doorstep, and Lisa is trying with futility to keep up her spirits. But she had seen the look on Alec's face. That look haunts her now. She walks to her kitchen, grabs a soda out of the fridge and listens to Cory and Justine in the other room, giggling, talking. She knows Karl will be there shortly, and she sighs, a void in her chest only echoing the void she feels around her. She walks to the couch, isolated, sits as the front door opens and Karl strolls in. No, she glances at him. He isn't strolling; he's swaggering.

He plops beside her, casually throws an arm around her shoulders. She shrinks, lowers her eyes. He asks what they want to do today and before Cory can answer, Lisa asks if he's heard from his brother.

Cory shakes his head. "Alec won't answer my calls."

She glances at them. Cory looks at her sternly, but with empathy. Justine looks on with pity. Karl just shakes his head, stands and holds out a hand. She looks up at him; he's smiling at her, softly, with eyes full of sympathy and something else that causes her to hesitate. There's something in his look that she doesn't trust.

"Can we go talk for a minute?" he asks, and after a brief glance to Justine and

Cory—both look bewildered at his actions—she takes his hand, cold and pale and freckled, and follows him out on the back stoop.

He looks concerned, shuffles around and seems like he's having trouble starting. He hangs his head, sighs, kicks at nothing and sighs again. Finally he begins.

"Alec isn't who you think he is."

She asks what he means, and sees what he's trying for, but the distrust is stronger than ever. She shakes.

"He took us to where you work, me and Cory. We saw Justine. We saw you. We were barhopping that night, I was the most sober so I was driving. And after we left we went to another bar and you were all Alec could talk about."

She smiles, can't help the smile, to know that he had been crushing on her so. But Karl looks at her gravely, and her smile drops.

"I told him you'd be a good woman to hold. He was really drunk by then, and Cory was just gone. He couldn't remember that night. Alec was loud and we had bumped into a few more people, so he was talking it up to quite a few of us. But you have to remember he was really drunk. So don't hold it against him."

She can't control the shaking now. "What did he say?"

"He said," he pauses, looks at her directly, "and I quote: 'Fuck that shit, man. I'd ride her all night long. I'd whip her around until she couldn't walk straight.'"

Something in her stomach gives, and she feels herself double over. She feels nausea, disbelief that Alec would say that. Karl rushes to her and puts an arm around her, touches her cheek with his cool hand and gazes into her eyes.

"I told him sex was useless, and it was more important to have a friend, but he insisted that all women were good for was what was between their legs. I'm sorry, Lisa."

She isn't sure why, but she begins to cry, and Karl holds her close. He kisses her forehead and she looks up at him. He kisses her lips and she doesn't pull away.

Karl pulls away, staring mystified as Lisa shakes her head and slides into the corner. She looks at him, sees more of that uncertainty underlining the compassion he's trying to exude, questions again all he told her. She tells him she isn't ready, she doesn't want to rush things, as she thinks about his arms snaking around her, his tongue probing, forcing its way between her lips. A hand moved to her hip and touched a thigh and tried for her ass, as the other moved up her side toward her breast. That was when she pulled away.

He says he thought she wanted him, and the compassion in his eyes is fading, turning lurid, and she tells him she needs some time alone. She is relieved that she doesn't have to spell it out, as he stands to leave. He looks mad, turns away, and stops before he opens her door. When he looks back that gentleness is back in his eyes.

"I'm sorry. I got over zealous. Look, I won't bother you for a day or two, but if its all right I'd like for the four of us to still go to the lake on Friday. I know you need time."

He starts to leave and she calls to him. Maybe there was something wrong with her that caused all men to walk away. Alec walked, and as she sits there, worrying that Karl is going to walk too, that thought crosses her mind. She is too young to accept it, though, so she pushes it away and tells Karl that he doesn't need to do all that. Yes, they'll still go to the lake on Friday.

As he leaves she sits in the room alone. She hears him say something to Cory, and as Karl's truck is pulling away, Cory enters. He looks at her, sits beside her, asks if anything is wrong. She shakes her head and won't speak.

"Something happening between you and Karl?" There is concern in Cory's voice; he is so similar to his brother, though neither sibling wants to see it.

"What happened that night you guys went out?"

He isn't sure which night she is referring to, so she tells him, at least Karl's version. Cory sits in silence, even after she's done. He bends his legs and folds his hands together, forearms on his knees, and calls for Justine. Justine enters, and Cory asks if Lisa will tell her what Karl said. All Justine can do is exchange a glance with Cory.

Cory speaks, finally. "Justine and I have been talking about Karl, hanging around so much now that Alec's gone. I told her about that same night just after he started coming by without Alec. Karl lied to you, Lisa."

Justine corroborates. Cory had told her this almost a day or two after they last saw Alec. Lisa hangs her head, the stress building in her neck and temples. She looks at them exasperated, asks what they should do.

Cory says they shouldn't kick Karl out of their lives yet. She should make it clear she just wants friendship with him, but don't let him know the truth.

"I feel like a whore," Lisa says, staring at the floor.

"Let's wait. We'll get Alec to come back, and let him know what happened. Karl is his friend—" the word friend rolls off Cory's tongue with as much disdain as he can muster—"Alec should be the one to deal with him."

Justine agrees, and Lisa, though she takes some convincing, realizes that is the best course of action. None of them know how long it will take for Alec to return, or that they'll never get to confront Alec with the truth about Karl, or that things will work out anyway, despite that.

Lisa collapsed on the couch, watched the clock, working and keeping time as though it had never stopped. She felt a chill, but still she sat there in the dark. Her imagination told her they could step from the shadows, or walk around the corner, and she shivered. She thought once about going to bed, then realized she'd sleep on the couch tonight, just as she had several nights ago. Then she had started awake from her bed, shaken by something—that alone frightened her—then felt compelled to walk into the living room. She fell asleep on the couch staring at the hummels, illuminated by an inconsistent, unnatural light. It wasn't moon light, and no artificial light existed outside, and nothing was on in the house. Still they had glowed.

Tonight, as her eyes grew heavy, she had a more sensible reason for sleeping out here. Alec was going to stay up all night. He would not rest, so neither would she. She would stay out here, in case he needed her for something tonight.

NINE
Lisa Remembers

Lisa had been determined that afternoon to climb the extension ladder with him and survey the roof. As they walked he grew more despondent, spoke with a defeated tone about the discolored tiles that had allowed moisture to enter and settle, rotting the boards underneath, dampening the insulation and sagging the sheet-rock below.

He collapsed in the recliner in the living room, leaned forward slowly and put his hands over his face. She watched him, felt the self blame wash over him, exuding from him to stifle the air in the room. He looked up and about and mumbled that they should call the electrician, even though he had a feeling what was to be found. Behind the house's façade of beauty, behind its décor, behind the mask of elegance with its stone facing, the oak trim, the brass knobs and sculpted banister railings—the house was dying. Night was settling quickly, coolly, and they could feel it creep through the cracked sealant around the windows. The kids' room was lit, the children nestled and silent, and she knew like the past three nights he'd rise to watch them till he was sure the shadows wouldn't move. She would watch him, and then when he finally trudged upstairs as dawn approached, she would go to bed.

He stared at the wall, unblinking. "We woke them up, you know."

She nodded. Taking a glance around the room, she tried to imagine all the problems that must be consuming him. "We'll fix the house."

"He'll get out eventually."

"He's not out yet."

Alec repeated her last word, his lips quivering as that word was the key. Yet. He shuddered. "You remember when I first brought you home from college?" he asked.

"I remember."

"My dad's friend was up for the weekend, with his wife." His dad's friend was, in fact, a blind musician—a jazz singer on the keys. He was white, to break the cliché, and muscular. His wife looked older than he—or maybe it had been that as a blind musician he held his age well—and she was very nice, a bit anal retentive, perhaps, but what less to expect when you had spent twenty years caring for someone with a disability. He talked quickly of how nice they were as a couple, and how talented he was as a musician. They both smiled at the impromptu neighborhood concert where the man performed with Will behind on a drum kit.

"My first and only jazz concert," Lisa said, her eyes bright.

"You liked it."

"No," she corrected him. "I loved it. I thought I was a rocker at heart."

They sat there for a moment, reminiscing, silent, their minds joined in another place where things were different; they were younger and freshly in love. Lisa remembered something else about the man's wife, something she had said. She had told her of her own marriage for twenty-five years, and she had looked at both of them when she continued talking.

"The key is to treat them as your best friend. In all that you say. In all that you do, treat them as your best friend. Be nicer to no one above them."

Alec stood but he didn't look at her. He looked at the walls, as though he could see the problems masked behind them. He paused in the hall to stare down to the kids' door, and what he was expecting she didn't know. He didn't wish her goodnight, didn't glance back at her, when he walked up the stairs. Lisa sat alone in the darkening house.

So much ground covered for them, she thought, *and so much more left to tread.* As the night closed in, his fears that kept him awake became hers, until to sit still and just think became unbearable. She had to stand, and so she stood in the dark, until that too wasn't enough and so she walked until she found herself in the laundry room. She stared to the wall next to her bedroom door, and to the door that led down into the basement. It was unlocked. She reached out, touched it; it creaked open. The stairwell light was on; it was still dark just beyond that, she asked herself if she had turned it off. She thought she had. She took the first step, put her hand against the white plaster wall, felt its roughness as she took two more down.

The door closed behind her.

From below static from a monitor called to her. She reached the bottom, could see the twenty-inch monitor snow under a blanket of dust, saw the bay window glass with black just beyond. The studio gear had never been moved from the layout Alec's father had accessed it, but unless Alec had flipped its switch in the fuse box, no power should be coming in here.

She walked toward the light switches by the VCRs, checked them for power and tapes and all were off and empty. She flipped on the lights for the console, checked the computers. Even the power strips were off. She imagined the fuse could be blown, asked how the monitor could still work, and the thought was cut off. She found herself sitting in the high back leather swivel, unable to move, when the static left and the first picture came up.

It looked like a home movie—his father had video taped a lot of them. Lisa could hear his father behind the scenes, laughing and moving the frames as Cory and Alec wrestled and squirted each other with water guns. They got their mother a few times, laughing. It was the day of the last picnic they ever had. They had swam in the numbing river, nearly went into shock with the contrast of the heat of day. They had eaten and laughed, and like every visit they made a ritual of stopping by to see Grandpa on their way home. Alec had told her about this day, its effect on him so great it even impacted her. She could see it as clearly in her head as the pictures on the monitor. Their parents were afraid the man had pneumonia, but he swore it was a cold from under his three Afghans, the house stagnant from lack of A/C. It had been pneumonia, they discovered, as they walked through the door. Alec ran in first, all of ten, calling for his grandfather, finding him on the couch in the living room. Alec wasn't sure what passed was, and had only a theoretical knowledge of death when he walked into the living room that day, thinking his grandfather was asleep.

He shook the old man, as his parents and Cory followed, shook again and froze. That was the first time Alec had seen a body devoid of life. He never went to the visitation. He wouldn't go to the church service, and his mother stayed with him. She convinced him that the casket would be closed at the graveside service, but he never left the car. He waited for them, biting his nails and watching, on the verge of tears.

His father's grave countenance made no effect on him, when they joined up. He stared at his oldest son, and Alec could only look at the fresh mound of dirt piled in front of the tombstone.

"You should have paid your last respects," his father had said.

At ten, Alec wasn't sure what that really meant. He could only think of one thing. "I touched him," he said.

On screen, Alec had just pushed his little brother into the creek. Cory jumped out, looking like a mongrel dog, shaking off water. Alec laughed on screen and then it faded to black. There was screaming.

Lisa was laid back, her legs up, her body glistening; she screamed again and Alec watched, full view of more of her than he had seen in a while. He watched his son birthed, first the head then shoulders—a sympathy pain shot through his groin and he cringed—and then the baby slid out, umbilical cord and all. He stepped on screen long enough to hold a pair of snips while the doctor cradled the crying infant, severing the physical tie between mother and son. He handed the snips to the nurse, knelt by his wife. Lisa was red-faced and panting. Alec hugged her. "We have a son," he whispered on screen.

"William Thomas Bradshaw," she mumbled, remembering the words and how he had said them that night. "We'll call him Billy."

"Two Years Later" flashed, and Billy was a toddler. Alec was rocking him. Such a scene had happened many nights, but Lisa knew where this was leading. It was the night his mother and father had gone to bed. Will had been fighting some rash of symptoms since before

Lisa's pregnancy. This night Billy didn't want to sleep, and it was almost midnight when Alec finally got him down. At that time Alec's mother had casually rolled over, her consciousness trapped between alert and asleep. She felt her husband's bare chest, cold. She called Alec first—waking Billy to tears—then called the ambulance.

She was in the waiting room when Alec had arrived. He called Cory, consoled her a little till the doctor emerged, his face hanging, sorrow in his eyes. Alec entered alone. He stared at his father, eyes closed, pale. He walked over and took his father's hand. There was no movement. He knelt and bowed his head, closed his eyes. His mother was sniffling when she entered, the tears coming silently now. She was leaning on Cory's shoulder. Alec only noticed them when they rested hands on his shoulder. His only sign of acknowledgment was an extension of legs, and standing between them he put an arm around each. They stood around the bed, no one speaking, watching their father in his final sleep.

Lisa watched the screen fade from the hospital scene to black; she lowered her head, sniffed, and raised her eyes again as a new picture came into light. It was an exterior shot of an old wooden house with a tin roof, surrounded by long-leaf yellow pines, mosquitoes buzzing, even on screen the August air was thick. The film was grainy, showing them as college kids, five of them walking into the house.

"Don't go in," she whispered as the door closed behind them.

The video played on, jumping from scene to scene, ending with a frame shot that looked like it had been paused. She didn't want to look. A girl was on the stairs, grinning into the camera. Shadows engulfed her, watched her and watched the camera, staring with sanguine eyes, her own lurid. She had been dead some fifty years, by the time this footage was shot. And at this point in the film, Lisa knew the girl had been gone, replaced by whatever they had awakened.

The monitor clicked off, leaving her in darkness. She looked over her shoulder to the dark basement, the stairs. It was cool. She didn't want to move, so she stayed there all night, reliving the past and contemplating the future.

At first light, her eyes fluttered and she looked to her surroundings with drowsiness. The studio was dimly lit, an alien glow from the intruding dawn making it a shocking place to awaken. But as her mind came to it brought the nights events: Alec's fears and relived memories caged by video, shown through equipment that should no longer work—dreams, she tried to shake them off; but they weren't dreams. And with that understanding she stood. She didn't run.

The ghosts were real. She looked around. There sat his father's drum kit, disassembled last night into its components, hardware piled together, the toms and snares and kick-drum cluttered in a group and the cymbals packed into their travel bag—now it was assembled. The hardware stood and held the drums, supported the kick drum and housed the cymbals and the drum kit was ready to be played again. Through the vents she could hear the distant ticking of a clock that hadn't worked in years, keeping time now. The ghosts were real.

Alec's fears were real. There was so much ground between them. And would they be together again, as they were, when Karl was released? It was no longer a question of "if," for either her or Alec. Karl would return, and the shadows would move. The legend was slow to return to her; it was something she hadn't thought of in years. But when its pieces just began to assemble her pallor dropped and her lips tightened and grayed. She could hear a faint echo, separated from her by seven years, still chilled enough to remind her it had been the worst sound she had ever heard. And there was something else. She began to shake. This house, built and standing on memories now, would lose more than the ghosts that walk the halls. Her legs gave and she started to sit down in the chair. She caught herself. She looked past the studio into the still black basement, the faint outline of stairs leading up catching her eyes. Without a pause she stood again; without slowing she stepped, transcended the risers until she passed through the laundry room—she locked the door behind her— and then she was in the kitchen.

She walked to the counter and pulled open a middle drawer that should serve little purpose. This drawer didn't hold utensils, or rags or hand towels—small storage bowls with lids weren't to be found. It was the most basic of utility drawers, found in most kitchens. It held a few screws. It held a screwdriver and a pair of scissors. There may have been a sticky pad, a few pens, but she bypassed all that. She pulled from the back of the drawer a black velvet box that hadn't been opened in over a year. It had been buried in anger, pushed to where she could be sure it wouldn't be in the way again. She lifted it in the palm of one hand, and with the other she brushed off the dust. Then she opened it.

When they first met, as they got to know each other, Alec had asked her many questions, one of which was about her heritage. Pale as she was in that early spring—when it still required some kind of jacket to go outside—she told him she tanned easily in the summer. That she attributed to the Cherokee in her. The rest, the most was Irish. When he returned from his three month absence, on a day when it was just the two of them, before they went on their road trip, he had produced the box sitting on her countertop now, allowed her to open it. The crest on the ring, he told her, was Celtic—Irish. "It means," he said, "the hands that hold the heart that crowns the relationship." Above the heart was a crown, she imagined the carving representative of something with which a Celtic prince adorned his temple, jewel encrusted, gold. This was Sterling. She had hugged him tightly.

She removed the Claddagh ring, examined it—spots had begun to dull, the luster tarnished and fading—and then she put it back in the box. She stuck it back in its spot in the drawer, pushed it closed and leaned against the counter.

She had been to see Karl once since that night, when the shadowfolk were awakened. He was at the halfway house; she caught him in between his trips to rehab and to the hospital and found him resting. A fingertip brushed the surface of the drawer's face, and she recited its meaning under mumbled breath. She had gone back to Karl not for closure, for his deception. She had not seen him because of any dormant feelings. She had simply found a videotape Alec had tried to hide. Watching it, she saw more than just them at the house, awakening the shadows. She realized why Alec had hidden it, and now only Karl had the answers.

He hunkers over in his chair, hiding his bulging eyes. She feels no need to tell him of their personal lives, so she waits. When he looks at her she is frightened, but tries not to show it. He speaks and it is as though he is already beaten.

"I won't let them turn out the lights, here. Not even at night. I don't see them as much when the lights are on."

Her voice trembles a little, but she works through that. "What was that I saw on the tape?"

"That poor little girl," and his eyes look far away, to a place she can't see. He smiles, brings his gaze back to her, chuckles a little. "She was probably our age when she died, though. Or close. But she wasn't jail bait, I don't think."

He looks around the room, seems to grow frightened. He tries to shrink back from something, just over him, and when he speaks to her again he does so in hurried tones.

"It's part of their tricks really. They make you think you still see the ghosts. But they've already eaten the ghosts. The spirits make them strong enough to get what they really want."

She rubs a hand over her stomach absently. She asks what they really want and his head falls, his body slumps. He doesn't speak for several minutes, and when he does she decides she wants to leave.

"They've promised me you, if I give them what they want. I could have been with you, you know. It's Cory's fault, and Justine's, and even Alec's. But don't worry. They'll get theirs, and I'll have you."

He is leering at her, his eyes red and darkly rimmed. "Can you see them, Lisa? They see you. They see all of you. They are promising me things, Lisa. Telling me things." He looks not at her breasts, nor her face, nor her legs. He looks at her flat stomach. "If I only give them what they want."

She leaves without saying anything else.

Coffee burped at her, brought her back to the new day. She couldn't remember getting it ready, and that's because she hadn't. She glanced across the bar to the breakfast table; Alec sat in the chair, his back to her, his elbows spread over the table like wings enveloping a nest. Steam rolled in front of him, up past his head, and she couldn't believe she had been so engrossed in her own memories that she didn't see him come through. He had to have stood less than two feet from her. He had to have turned on the water faucet, and reach around her to get the grounds sealed in their own ceramic canister. And yet she hadn't seen him.

He stood and walked around the table, entered the kitchen and looked at her. He held his own cup, his arm bent at a right angle, still except for the rolling steam out of the cup. He stared at her, blinked once, asked her if she had been up all night.

She nodded. "Just thinking."

He shifted. "Coffee's ready, if you want a cup." He looked away, toward the living room, looked as though his vision could turn corners and show him what he couldn't possibly see. "Kids will be up soon I guess."

She nodded again, watched him walk away; the stairs reverberated with his footsteps. She poured herself a cup, trembling a little, waiting for the sun to rise a little higher, remembering one more thing that happened to them seven years ago.

When Alec had returned to her collegiate existence, they had done many things together, just the two of them. He took her to movies and to a couple of football games when the season started—that was after their road trip, though—and on a picnic and they went swimming. Many nights they had to wait till after he closed the store before taking her out, and one such night he changed the plans abruptly. He locked up, but they were still inside. He dutifully checked the lights and secured the cash and the till, and then he led her to the back.

She hadn't come to believe in ghosts that night, but his interest in them became hers, as her own curiosity was piqued.

Thinking about that now, sipping coffee, she remembered how she felt with him then. It had been the perfect combination of a romantic relationship and a deep and abiding friendship. Like the spirit that night, who not thirty minutes later began shuffling and fixing shelves of books that Alec had intentionally disorganized, there relationship was something supernatural then. But, she theorized, since ghosts exist in nature, supernatural couldn't be a good word. Nor could it fit them, and as she tried to find an appropriate word, she watched him move and go about a normal routine that every adult does in the morning, as they wake. She found herself smiling, at his commonplace movements, and recognized that the feeling was returning.

TEN
Claddagh and Closure

He had been in the principal's office for ten minutes, had left her in the front lobby, and she assumed all was going well. With any luck they'd set up an appointment with the superintendent and then the school board, and Alec could come back. Those were her hopes, anyway, as she waited. They would need the money, soon. Billy was ready to start kindergarten and that meant school supplies and lunches. Montessori didn't give discounts to teachers, and for another two months tuition for both children would run nearly sixteen hundred dollars. At least that would be cut in half for Kimber, starting August. But Alec's profitable adventure of hunting ghosts could barely assist her in the bills. And with him home, as nice as it was, there weren't a lot of ghosts to catch in this town.

She read the maroon banner flung over the crème colored wall, discarded it and looked at the floor. She saw enough of these lockers nine months out of the year, read enough banners and attended enough school functions. She didn't want to be here today. The front door opened and she watched a tall woman a little on the dumpy side, juggling a briefcase and a few paper sacks, her keys jangling. One sack began to fall and Lisa caught it, smiling, helping to brace the load enough that the woman even had a free hand to wipe a matted bang from her forehead. She puffed.

"Mrs. Kubrick? What are you doing here?"

The Spanish teacher smiled and flexed her linguistic muscles. *"Voy*

129

a ponerse al dia con uno trabajo."

Lisa blushed; it had been a while for her. The teacher told her she was here catching up on some work, added she was teaching a Spanish class for the second summer term, confided that half the students were seniors that would have been gone in May and then rolled her eyes. No one could be more accused of letting a child slide than Mrs. Kubrick, and Lisa knew some of those kids would not have to come back. She turned and looked at the closed principal's door, even as Mrs. Kubrick asked her about her presence with summer in full swing.

Lisa felt herself blushing again, dropped her eyes. "Alec came home."

The woman's jubilee was barely contained, and Lisa thought the entire load was going to spill to the floor. It nearly did, but Lisa caught another bag and helped to stack the things again in Mrs. Kubrick's arms. Alec had made a lot of friends during his short tenure, all of them sad as his family began to pass, sadder yet when they learned he was leaving.

"So you two are back together?"

Rather than say sort of, "we're working on it, we've hashed things out once and now we're trying to rebuild our relationship" and ramble on with such details, Lisa—still blushing—nodded. The woman was begging for a hug, so Lisa gave her one. She tried to take a bag as the teacher pulled away, then said something. Lisa stared at her, mouth agape. She asked her to repeat it, only received a look of shock from Mrs. Kubrick.

"I just said I'm so happy for you two. It was all such a tragedy."

Lisa nodded absently, her mind reeling from what she thought she heard. Mrs. Kubrick asked and Lisa tried to laugh her off, said she's had a lot on her mind and it really was nothing. Mrs. Kubrick smiled and said again how happy she was, then realized what Lisa was doing here. She asked if Alec was coming back and Lisa shrugged. That was their hope, she said, and with that Mrs. Kubrick smiled. She glanced up to the clock and her smile dropped. She turned down the long hall, saying she hated to run, well wishing and smiling and attempting a wave. Lisa smiled, waved, thought again of what she had heard.

"Hacimos ruidos por la noche."

"We make noises through the night," she said, and by now her attention focused elsewhere. To the banner, where in bold caps was the team name—WILDCATS—and beside it, written in thin script—Catch the Spirit!

The principal's door opened and Alec walked out, trying to look upbeat, looking instead like a sophomore just given a month's detention. She didn't have to ask what had been said.

"They'll use me for a substitute. The board is happy with the guy that replaced me. Principal Dick in there had the cahonas to confide with me that they really just want to test me." He slammed the lobby door open and walked out into the sun; Lisa followed, wanted to remind him that he had run off, instead caught up with him.

"It's better than chasing ghosts for a living," she said, glanced up at him and met his eyes. "It's a start."

He sighed and shrugged, looked up to the sunlight and brought a smile back down to her. "I guess I deserve it."

"No you don't," and her voice was tender. He sighed, dropped his eyes, only to raise them when he felt her fingers curl around his. It was a brief touch, ending with a hearty shake and a suggestion that they retrieve the kids to play. He agreed and she let go and walked ahead, bouncing lightly, her hair blowing. She cocked her head back and smiled at him, and nothing else was said as they climbed in the car and drove to the daycare.

Nearly a month after their argument—less a climax than Alec had hoped for—he watched Lisa chase the kids across the yard and bounce and play. He saw his inadequacies as he watched them. There was too much distance still between him and his wife, and that very distance left his judgement foggy. He spent too much time second-guessing how she'd react when all he wanted was to hold her again. That was the next bridge to cross—to spend a night in her arms again, holding her tight in one bed.

He heard Billy ask his mommy to spin him around; she shook her head, she just didn't have the energy. In exaggerated movements he turned and flapped his arms and squinted ... and then he caught sight of his father. Alec's arms were extended before Billy could even ask him.

Kimber and Lisa watched as Billy gave Alec his arms, leaned from his father. The two began to turn, Alec in place and Billy running sideways to keep up. Alec spun faster. Billy's feet began to skip, and then left the ground totally. Alec leaned away from him, tucked his elbows into his sides and held tight. Billy's feet were level with his head, and his laugh was rich like a field of grass after the first spring rain. Alec slowed, tasting the early dinner roast beef as it bubbled up from his stomach, the world spinning, slowed more and Billy's feet began to drop. As the feet hit the ground Alec stopped spinning but the world didn't. He tried for balance, doubled over and caught Billy's shoulder as the boy tried to walk straight to his mother. Somehow he made it to his wife, felt her hands on his shoulders as she tried to steady him. The world around him slowed but he was still out of breath and lightheaded. *What would happen*, he wondered, *when Billy and Kimber were all grown up?* She held him straight, smiling at him as Billy continually rammed into her side, feigning the dizziness by now. This what was happening now, was only possible with the children around. She tried to wave her son off, to get him to quit running into her as he giggled. Without the kids to bring the happiness, Alec realized, straightening, sobering, he and Lisa may divorce later. They may just quit talking. He had seen old couples like that, only snapping the few times they spoke to each other.

He felt a tug on his shirt, and so he looked down.

Kimber was smiling up at him, looking so much like Cory with that glint in her eye. "Spin me, Uncle A."

He sighed.

Alec took a seat on the porch after both kids spun; each wanted to go again, screamed at him with joy that they be spun—"Make me dizzy, Daddy!" Billy cried—but Lisa had taken one look at his face and suggested they join her on the trampoline. He sat and watched them, smiling, his stomach jumping with them until he had to turn his eyes away. The mimosa was still bare but ready to bloom as August neared, and it was easy for him to see the mockingbird land on its branches and watch them. He smiled. A refuge pet from his grandmother's life in the house, it still came around, though neither he nor Lisa had adopted her old habit of feeding it. It watched them now, called as a Blue Jay and somewhere far off there was an answer. It cocked its head to the children, sang a sparrow's song. Alec smiled.

He turned his attention back to his family, his smile broadening as the children laughed. Lisa seemed so graceful with them, her perky breasts bouncing and giving him rise. He looked back at the bird as giddiness fluttered with his uneasy stomach, and watched it lift into the air, flutter in place, lower itself back to the branch and call out. He laughed at the warped connections his mind formed. He turned his attention back to his family, got lost in them as they climbed off the trampoline, and then the bird did something wholly unexpected.

It buzzed them. It perched on the frame of the swing set, called to them, fluttered up. Alec cocked his head as the children and Lisa took notice. Billy laughed and took a step back, closer to his mother. Kimber smiled and shifted nervously, and Alec—unfamiliar with the behavior of birds—watched close at it lifted off and flew just above their heads again.

All three jumped; Billy swatted and Kimber shook her head and the bird landed in a nearby oak. It called to them again as a Whippoorwill, flew and hovered, landed, sounded eerily like a cardinal when it talked to them again and then flew to buzz them again. It didn't come as close this time and so they didn't jump, but watched in awe as the bird flew away.

They walked back to the porch and Alec stood, something his stomach wasn't ready for so he swayed a little, caught himself and straightened. He offered a smile through the queasiness. Lisa patted his shoulder and glanced over her shoulder with a quizzical look. He had lost sight of the bird, and could only shrug before opening the door to let them back into the house. The tick of the clock greeted them—

something they had already grown accustomed to—as did something new that stopped Alec as he noticed. He grabbed Lisa's shoulder so quickly she jumped, and didn't mean to bark when he ordered the kids to go get a bath. She looked at him and furrowed her brow at the look on his face. Then she followed his eyes.

The hummels on the mantle were bathed in the dimness of the early evening, and glowed in an ethereal light inconsistent with the rays of the sun. Alec stepped toward them and felt Lisa take hold, pull him back. She squeezed his hand and he swallowed, a sound that surely resonated in her ears because it echoed through his own. There were no words for him, watching the light, and a thousand questions he dared not voice. It all came down to one undeniable fact they both understood, and one question they truly wished they didn't already know how to answer.

The activity was increasing, though they were slowly growing closer together. Why?

The answer came as an aria from the mockingbird, back again and just outside their window. And then the hummels exploded.

He broke her grasp and stepped forward as the room grew darker, more silent. He felt her near, take his hand again, and then he felt something else. He turned, looked over his shoulder, saw silhouettes and shapes unrecognizable in this little light. He felt it though, no matter where he looked, and felt it still as his attention was drawn back to the shattered figurines. He felt them watching through the darkness, eyes on him and not Lisa's, because her gaze was directed at the fireplace mantle. She passed him, knelt over the figurines, surveying them, and still he felt someone watching so hard, they prickled the hair on his arms and the back of his neck, like a cool breeze just caressing the skin. And they were right behind him.

Without turning he reached to the wall, felt along the paper till he came to hard plastic, and a little switch pointing down. He flicked it up and bathed the room in light, and only then did he turn. A hallway with only a grandfather clock met him, ticked at him. He sighed and faced his wife, then joined her in cleaning up the fragments.

Two days later and they still hadn't discussed the accident, but she could see it was weighing on him. Everything was weighing on him. He picked at his sandwich, stared and saw nothing, his eyes glassy and unblinking. He popped a chip into his mouth and crunched it, took a sip of water and looked up at her. She smiled, asked herself what they were doing. Lisa tried to imagine how he was on the cases, what he must have done to be so successful, as she watched him. It came to her then, as she thought he looked now as so many of his clients must have looked. She spoke, asking him how the rest of his day was planned. He shrugged and said he didn't know, asked her the same.

"Let's pick up the kids early. But first I want you to come with me."

"Where?"

She couldn't say it was a surprise. While he'd be unaware of the destination, maybe even shocked, surprise denoted the wrong emotion. "Just come with me," she said, and left it at that.

He had guessed it as she walked out of the flower shop. She asked him to wait in the car, and then he watched her walk out with a half dozen long stem red roses. She laid them in the backseat and climbed behind the wheel, watching him bite his fingernails and mutter something about the expense and then she drove. Alec was silent, even after they passed through the wrought-iron gate and turned down one of the single-lane paved roads winding amid the well-manicured grass. She stopped, pulled off the road a little and shut the car off, and without a noise he got out and grabbed the roses. As she walked around the side he tried to hand her a few but she wouldn't take them, only saying they were for him. He looked over to six concrete monuments and looked back at her.

"You came back for closure, right?"

"That's part of the reason," he said. She led him to the graves; they stopped in front of his mother's.

He looked down, set the rose in the brass vase at the foot of the headstone, saying nothing for a long time. A wind had picked up, cooling the hot July day, cooling the sweat on their brow. She touched his shoulder as he bowed his head.

"I'm sorry, Mom, for leaving them. Thank you for all you taught me."

He moved over one. The headstone listed his father's name, his date of birth and death. Alec set the rose in a similar vase and apologized for not closing with Grandpa all those years ago, and then thanked his father for being the man he was. The next was his grandmother's. He spent just as long at hers as he had his parents, asking for forgiveness, thanking her, setting the rose down. His grandfather was next, and then came Justine. He didn't stay as long at her grave. When he stood over Cory's, though, he knelt. He set the rose carefully in the vase, looked up into the sunlight and closed his eyes. Lisa watched him, rubbed his neck and ran her hand over his head.

"We'll take care of her, Cory," he promised, and he looked at the grave. When he stood over his mother's grave Lisa had thought she saw a tear in his eye. Now she saw one build, and it rolled down his cheek. He was silent; he backed away and stood in front of all the graves, and then he put his arm around his wife.

"I love you," he said to the headstones.

But I'm his life now, she thought, *the children are his life now.* His eyes washed over them, settled—Lisa assumed—on the grave of his grandmother. "I'm sorry about your hummels."

A cry out pulled Lisa from sleep that night, relieved her from her own nightmare that as she awoke, left her shaking. She grabbed her bearings and began to rise from her bed, even as amplified footsteps descended the stairs. She started to ask herself if Alec was awake already, when her mind brought her back to something far more important. Billy had screamed.

She pulled her robe closed as she exited the library and joined Alec at the door to the children's room. Billy was sweating, shaking and curled in his bed, his eyes dark and sunken and staring at a spot on the floor, staring at nothing. Alec beat her to him, wrapped his arms around his son and cradled Billy against his chest as Kimber awoke, upset from the commotion. Lisa tried to comfort the girl as she watched her son tremble, heave sighs. She looked at Alec as he stroked his son's shoulder, rocked him gently, kissed his forehead and reassured Billy in hushed tones that they were all there. Beyond that no one spoke, not even Kimber, who watched on. Surprisingly the first to speak up was Billy, and then he didn't look at anyone. He spoke quickly and softly, his voice broken from fresh use after rest, and sounding as he looked: hollow.

"My throat hurts, Daddy. I had a nightmare."

"Want me to get you some water?" Alec asked, and Billy shook his head, pressed it against his father's chest.

Lisa felt herself tremble, watching her son, thinking what she assumed Alec must have been thinking a few nights ago when the hummels exploded.

"It's all right now," she said, and both Alec and Billy looked up at her. She didn't even believe herself, from the sound of her own voice.

"I love you, Mommy," Billy said, and Alec squeezed him tight. She offered to get him some water, and in a hoarse tone he said he was better now.

All was silent again. The kids began to settle, and slowly Billy's trembling eased, his staring, vacant eyes began to blink and glaze, and he let out several yawns. Kimber stretched back and Lisa stood, covering her, kissing her cheek. She stepped to her son, tucked him though Alec had covered him already, kissed his forehead and felt a little too much warmth. She stepped back and glanced at Alec's face, saw the deep lines, the pain in his eyes. They stood in the doorway for a moment before pulling the door closed and walked back to the stairs. They faced each other, and Lisa was surprised a little to find themselves embraced, staring into the other's eyes.

Alec sighed; she felt his breath. Nothing seemed real in the dark anymore, not even his touch. The only proof she had was from what carried over into the sunlight, like the shards of ceramic they spent three hours sweeping off the mantle and picking out of the carpet. But more like a dream Alec pulled away, gave her another sigh and let his fingers linger to hers, reaching, as he stepped up the risers. As they parted he turned, still moving slowly, not looking back till he reached the top, and then it was only a pause before opening the door. As it closed she squeezed her arms, still waiting at the bottom in the dark.

Lisa walked down the hall until again she found herself at the brink of the children's room. She pushed the door open slowly, peering first with her head, then stepping into the closet light, eclipsing it and so disrupting the children. Neither woke. She crouched by Kimber's bed, and with gentle fingers caressed the little girl's hair as her eyes fell on the locket. It wasn't until Kimber stirred and rolled that Lisa stood and stepped back to the door. She watched both kids, checked the shadows and smiled down at their sleeping faces, so restful, and making everything else seem so absurd. It was then her decision to expedite the relationship with Alec, and the best way she understood was to let him see her with it on again.

She walked to the kitchen, opened the drawer and looked around the darkened house. All was silent; all was deep. From its recesses she pulled out the black jewelry box, flipped it open and returned the Claddagh ring to her finger. She held her hand up to the moonlight, examining it, frowning; it still looked naked. The ring finger was empty. She lowered her left hand, turned and leaned on the counter, and felt the loneliness of a sleeping house.

THE
SHADOWFOLK

ONE

A Call from Shag's Ferry

The director of Shag's Ferry Halfway House didn't know what commotion would be caused by his phone call; he thought he was doing Karl a favor. A surprise would be nice, but he felt that Karl's need to surprise his friends was undermined by the importance of letting them know.

Sitting in his office just large enough for an old wooden desk, the varnish fading, and a creaky office chair with holes in the cushion, the stuffing protruding, and staring at the cracked and faded crème plaster, he picked up the phone and dialed.

It wasn't hard to track them down. Every visitor to the house had to give their name and contact information, and both Alec and Lisa had listed the same address and given their real names. The address listed in the logbook was outdated, but there was a forward. Directory assistance gave him the number willingly, and while he surmised neither adult would be home in the middle of the day, he still called. They'd have an answering machine, he figured. As the phone rang, he sitting in a chair still reeking of cigarettes from the person who donated it, he began to have second thoughts. What if they weren't home? Didn't this warrant telling someone and not a machine? A feeling of urgency swelled within him, like this was more serious than he had imagined. He still hadn't considered Karl's last interview a ruse. Now he did and dropped the phone. On the other end Alec had picked it up to the sound of a thud. The cord had bungeed, the receiver bounced off the faded tile, slapped it again, swung a little then dragged. The director snatched it up and hung up the phone.

How dangerous this man, if it was a ruse. If this past six months were all a game, and he still believed the shadowfolk were real. In his legend the shadowfolk went after children, and he had stated many times at the beginning that he and Lisa were meant to be together. The director bit his knuckle, then did two things he'd sworn off completely.

The first was light a cigarette. One of the night guards consistently left his pack in the drawer, a constant temptation. He took a drag and to his surprise he didn't cough, though it had been five years since he had last lit one. The second he did after leaving a message for the evening nurse who kept watch before the guards came. He told her he was going home early. He was sick. He'd see her tomorrow. Then he drove to a bar.

What scared him as the beer filled his stomach, washed out his mouth and the taste of the cigarette, was what if Karl was right. Everyone had ghost stories, every town had its local legend and every family had an uncle or grandmother or sibling that refused to move on, banged pots and pans in their kitchen or turned on lights or moved things. His own family had stories; at more reunions than he could count family members tried to debunk his psychology by offering up tales—most they had witnessed—and dared him to demystify them. Some he could, some he had to stretch his own beliefs in order to rationalize. He had never seen a ghost, but he had known a few people even in the halls of academia that had. By three o'clock that afternoon he had had enough alcohol to convince himself that ghosts—especially the shadowfolk—were real. By five he realized he had to drive home, and began ordering coffee. By the end of happy hour the bartender had returned his keys, begrudgingly, and the director of the Shag Ferry Halfway House left, bought a case of beer at a nearby liquor store, and drove home.

Everything was still a blur as he dialed the number again, but the case rested unopened in his refrigerator. He felt sick, as only one could feel when they sobered up too quickly after drinking so heavily, not giving the alcohol time to wear itself out of their system. The phone was answered, he asked for Alec or Lisa and the male voice on the other end—sounding distorted, almost grainy—said they were out with their children. He contemplated asking if this were Karl, but the voice wasn't a familiar one, so he introduced himself then got straight to the reason he had called.

"Oh," the man's voice replied. "He said he was coming here?"

"He said he had nowhere else to go."

The man thanked him and hung up. The director hung up his phone, turned on the television, sighed. He took a few minutes to contemplate his actions, stood, and walked into the kitchen. There could be a sense of personal empowerment, amid all this, where he regained himself and beat his disease once again by throwing the unopened case into the trash. It could be dramatized by a steady action, as he took each beer, opened it, and poured it down the sink, tossing each empty can away. He was unmarried because his problem had ruined enough relationships and he had no strength left to try for companionship anymore. His family long gone, so any sign of strength would only be there for him and God to see. He apologized to his higher power, removed his ten-year sobriety coin from his pocket, recited the Lord's Prayer and the Serenity Prayer, and took the first beer from the fridge. He opened it and drank it quickly, then grabbed the second.

The sickness began to dwindle; he continued into the night.

TWO
Hopes and Wishes

Alec hung up the phone and found himself trembling. That had been the day before, when the man identifying himself as the director of the halfway house where Karl had been staying called, saying that Karl had been released. Today he had a mission.

Alec snapped the bolt shut then tested the window. The bay windows would be a problem. They were too big, the storm windows that helped secure them were held in place only by pegs screwed into holes. If they wanted to get in bad enough, they could through there. *If they wanted to get in bad enough*, he reasoned, *they could follow Karl down through the chimney*. Alec had been in the basement for two hours, checking every outlet, every window—even the ones such as the bay windows that didn't open—making sure the lock on the garage was secure and testing the studio door and the basement door. He searched for large holes and cracks in the foundation, and only depressed himself more. None were large enough for Karl to wriggle in from the outside, or hide in if he breached the house's exterior, but there were large cracks. He knelt by one just on the other side of the stairwell, down the L-turn that ended in an old bathroom with spotted toilet and a sink collecting rust on the basin and a thick deposit of lime on the faucet. The crack went from the floor to the ceiling, seemed to disappear into the ceiling where the plaster was spider-webbed and flaking. He ran his hand along the powdery wall, feeling the crack—there were so many cracks like this one, and some worse—and a thought occurred to him then. This house was not just sheltering the ghosts of his past. This house had long since died, and was a ghost itself.

He examined his fingertips, recalling the girl curled up in her bed in Georgia, how flaked and dry her skin had been, like the falling plaster of this room. The cracks brought more memories, worse memories, and two words synonymous with the awakening of the shadowfolk— cracked mirrors. The walls, the ceilings in his basement now looked just like the mirrors that night, before they exploded and the shadowfolk came, and swallowed the ghosts.

There was no question in Alec's mind as to what he had to do. As Lisa readied the children to take them to school this morning, he had been working it out in his head. 1) Karl was a threat that had to be eliminated, if his family were to be safe; 2) The shadowfolk could not get the children, no matter what, and if Karl were dead, then a) the shadowfolk would need someone to latch onto, and b) Lisa was not an option. 3) The only way to destroy the shadowfolk came when they were attached to a person, or had possessed them as they had the caretaker in Georgia, and to do that 4) You had to destroy the person. There was no other choice. The shadowfolk were coming, and Karl was bringing them.

He walked up the stairs and poured a glass of water, then sat at the kitchen table. The sun was warm and bright and did much to fight the air conditioner. The humidity was seeping in, and Alec felt sticky. He tugged at the breast of his t-shirt, wiped matted hair from his forehead and found some of the plaster had fallen on him. His mind was empty, and he listened to the silence of the house. Even the hum of the air conditioner and the grandfather clock's incessant need to keep time again couldn't rattle the overwhelming stillness. When it all became unbearable he did what he could to activate his thoughts, and tear away from the loneliness.

"I'd like to hold her again," he told the house. "If it has to end like this I'd like to hold her again. Just once."

Silence. Humidity. Cold and Hot. That was his answer, along with the steady tick of the pendulum swing of a dead clock.

The phone rang.

He cocked his head, realized it must be Lisa and wondered why'd she call. Maybe they decided to stay in town and wanted him to join them. Maybe it wasn't even Lisa.

It rang again.

He stood, raised his hand to the receiver and found it shaking. Maybe it was that doctor again. Maybe it was Karl.

It rang a third time and his hand, shaking worse than ever, pulled it off the cradle and pulled it toward his ear. He said hello to static and beneath, far beneath the steady electronic snow, he heard a voice that hadn't spoken in years. He heard his mother say his name, over and over again and her voice rose above the static until he slammed the phone back on the cradle and backed away, staring at it. His head shook in disbelief, and he stared. The phone began to ring again.

He lifted it off the receiver and slammed it down again. He didn't have to hold it to his ear to hear the static—louder this time—or the distortion of her voice. He had barely let go of the phone when it began a third time, ringing, the rings faster and a thought came to him.

Wide-eyed he ran to the den as the phone rang twice, then a third time. He tried to remember if they had set the machine to pick up on four or five rings and it didn't matter, it must have been four because he heard it click on and heard Lisa asking the caller to leave a message at the sound of the beep and he didn't want a message left because he didn't want to hear the voice. He grabbed the cord to the answering machine and ripped it out of the wall. The cordless was still connected at the base, and it spilled to the floor. He dropped the answering machine on the area rug that covered the hardwood floor and sat, sighing. He sank into the couch. He dropped his head and closed his eyes.

The phone rang again.

The kids were asleep—Billy out after fighting a sleepless night before and a fear he'd dream again—and Alec was upstairs writing. Lisa sat alone in the dark living room. Their return this afternoon had been steeped first in dread, then in worry, and since then her stomach rolled and her mind worked. Alec spoke little, seemed shaken, and wouldn't answer her about the phone mess in the den. The answering machine was busted and the cordless had been pulled and left on the floor, the base dangling. She fixed it, and without berating her husband she threw away the digital answering machine. She didn't yell at him because she understood. His mother had glued herself to the phone when alive. She called her children constantly and called her friends and called her husband and when the rare occasion came that there was no one to call, she checked her voice mail and left the cordless perched on her lap. It was always within reach—and so constantly always needing recharging, but she couldn't keep it on the base long enough to recharge it—and it was futile for anyone else to try and use the phone or connect to the Internet. Will, her husband, solved that problem. He got another phone line for the house and purchased DSL for the computer. After the deaths Alec—in an effort to be frugal—canceled the DSL and the second phone line. It made sense to Lisa, then, that in contacting them, this is the way his mother chose.

But that wasn't all that was bothering Alec. When they returned home he wasn't doing anything so dramatic as sitting in a chair in the den and rocking and staring at the phone. He was up, pacing the walls, pouring over the seals of the windows and doors and checking locks. He was investigating baseboards and running his hand along the cracks that splintered the walls beneath the wallpaper. More than the disarray of the phone system in the den, these actions worried her.

All afternoon this bothered her, and as night settled once again, and unreality became more than just a passing dream, became possible, her own fears worsened. She hadn't had the time to tell Alec, but his purpose for returning had become hers. She missed the nights when they snuggled under the covers, intertwined their legs and wrapped each other in their arms and kissed and said goodnight and fell asleep. She missed waking to his bed hair and puffy eyes that were—despite how tired he was—bright and the smile on his lips as he kissed her and they said good morning and squeezed each other close. All afternoon he had been evasive, and that caused her now to try and find what he must be planning.

Absently, as she reclined against the arm of the couch, she tugged at her lip. A deep swell of remorse brought sighs from her, and still she couldn't figure it out. It scared her. Worse than Karl's impending visit, even worse than what the shadowfolk could do, whatever was on his mind scared her.

She realized she felt the loss already, and asked the house for another way. Whatever his idea was, it was anything but a solution, because she knew she'd lose the kids despite it, and even him. In response the house groaned, and in remote dark corners pieces of plaster sprinkled down and clouded, like autumn drizzle. Intangible faces turned down as they set eyes on her, and from the darkness Cory watched, frowning, arms folded across his chest.

THREE
Karl on His Way

You had to take your time on the road, when you were just released. Karl understood that, mainly because they told him. He knew he couldn't go straight there because Alec and family would be expecting it. Because despite his best efforts, the director would call, and Karl would lose the element of surprise. So he had to wander some first. He had to let them stew and wonder, and even begin to relax. Because, he knew the Bradshaws would reason, if he didn't show immediately, he wasn't coming at all. Let the director's call fade from their memory. Let them lock their doors for a week or so, and check over their shoulders as they walked outside, and check windows for broken panes and closets for shadows. Let them stand outside the fence of the day care and watch their children play with others, and check their temperatures every time their little faces are flushed, and rush them to the doctor when they catch a sniffle. Then let them wait some more. Wait and start to forget to lock that door to the basement; wait and let them forget to check a pane of glass, open a closet door for just a coat. Wait and let them forget to keep all eyes on the children, to forget to watch them every night when they slept, to give them some Benadryl when they catch a sniffle and not take them to the doctor. Wait and let them forget, just enough—because let's be honest, neither Alec nor Lisa will ever forget completely—but they can forget just enough. If they forget just enough they'll slip, and when they start to slip he'll find that broken pane, and hide in the shadows and wait just a little more, till the shadowfolk eat.

149

He stopped in front of a diner, looked in briefly and caught his reflection in the afternoon sun. He was ragged and lean and hadn't eaten in days. At least they fed well at the halfway house, and he knew there was no time to eat. It was almost time to finish the last leg of his trek, and once that was done he'd have plenty of time to eat. Next door to the diner was another building with glass front, a larger building that housed a grocery chain predominant in the south, proudly displaying in script the phrase, "Associate Owned," and next to that, in bold-faced caps, "Open 24 hours." He smiled, jutted his hands into his pockets and felt the wad he had saved flipping burgers at the little barbecue stand three blocks from the halfway house. He always took a little home with him at night, and had begun to develop a paunch. He liked the weight, for a while, but it drained off nearly overnight when he learned he was getting out. Now his new larger pants fit loosely and he found himself wondering—as he passed through the automatic sliding door—if Alec would have a pair to fit.

He felt the eyes of patrons and workers as he walked down the aisle of fruits and vegetables and turned to make his way to the back of the store—they always kept them in the back. There was an old woman in a muumuu, her hair in a bun and dyed chestnut, staring from underneath her spectacles. A young man speckled with pimples ready to burst, wearing a long-sleeve white shirt and a black apron with gold lettering of the logo of the store, stared at him holding two cantaloupes. Karl smiled and waved at the boy, made like he was grabbing two cantaloupes down around his groin, continued walking. He found the glass booth encasing displays. There was a Magnum, a .45, rifles mounted on a turntable stood just behind an older man wearing a similar apron as the boy with the fruit. Karl knew he had to keep it simple.

He lowered an index finger to the glass top, never taking his eyes off the clerk. It fell squarely to a nine-millimeter pistol. The clip would hold nine, and one would be in the chamber. Just enough, they whispered. He shook his head.

"I want that one," and the clerk removed it from the case, began listing all the features he could have with it for just under three hundred dollars.

"Do you take cash?" and the clerk nodded, pointed out all the mechanical wonders of such a machine: accuracy, load time, hair-trigger.

"I suppose there's a seven day waiting period," and Karl realized he was keeping his cool. He dropped his eyes to the pistol, silver-polished and charcoal grip and the man let him hold it; it was cold, its weight thick and even, but not too heavy.

"No waiting period, the clerk told him. You got the cash and you can take it out of here today."

Karl wondered when Arkansas abolished the waiting period—or if they had—or even when it became a state issue and not federal law. He handed the cash over and realized that didn't matter.

He bought a box of shells and carried the box and all out to the parking lot, the eyes all on him. He had shown the man a valid driver's license. He had given the man cash.

He looked down the block to the bus stop, stopped at a steel-gray bullet trashcan with a flip-top lid, and removed the gun from his case. The gun he stuck in his pocket, the case he jammed in the trashcan. And then he heard them.

"Load the clip," they whispered. "Make sure there are enough shells in the clip and one in the chamber, save the others in your pocket and load the clip."

He removed the box of shells and the clip from the plastic shopping bag, opened the box and set the clip down. He knew in his wallet was just enough to get him a bus ride to Alec's hometown. *Or about two hundred miles in the opposite direction,* he thought. He counted the shells, looked up and realized he was sitting on the curb. They whispered a little louder, again what he should do. He loaded three shells.

He stopped. "I won't need ten," he whispered back to them.

They were screaming now, "Continue loading and get the damn thing full because you don't know what will happen."

He tossed the rest of the shells into the trashcan, stood, and examined the clip. He pulled the gun from his coat pocket and jammed the clip in its butt. He cocked it with the lever, sighted it there in the parking lot. Karl wasn't smiling anymore.

Returning the gun to his pocket, he began walking toward the bus stop. His head down, his eyes nearly shut, he was trying to ignore them as they yelled at him. But his head was beginning to throb and he suddenly realized the pain had never gone away. If anything, his years of trying to believe they weren't real had made the pain worse. They never let up, they never backed off when they promised; they only gave just enough to keep him going. *Well,* he thought, pushing their voices out, *what if we do this and she still won't come with me?* Alec wasn't so big it would take more than one bullet, and that would leave two. If she wouldn't join him.

FOUR
A Nightmare

Alec turned off the computer and rubbed his eyes, leaning over in his chair, he removed his glasses. He looked at the clock on the wall, the second hand invisible in the dimness of the room, the minute hand seemingly frozen. It was one-something, was all he could discern. He stood and felt his body sag, and quietly prided himself on concentrating on the writing for so long, without other thoughts drifting in. He was tired of the other thoughts, tired of the ticking clock and the hummels and the mockingbird and the phone calls and the cracking foundation. He wanted to see no more doors opening, no lights flickering; he wanted to feel no cold spots nor hear whispers from long dead voices. He didn't want to see the man with red hair, or the shadows with red eyes.

Alec stepped around the desk and moved to the bed, covered and laid down with a sigh. It was time to write when he could, to spend his free time with his wife and children and work on moving from this upstairs bed back to his nocturnal bridal carriage. It was time to play substitute at the public school for a while, until he had earned back their trust, and he could be on staff again. His eyes closed and he nestled himself under the covers, making a mental note to check at the local paper tomorrow for correspondent positions—or even a staff opening, he hoped—anything to bring in some more money. The crawl toward sleep came easily, and Alec realized it was time not for ghosts and legends, but for his family.

He sat up. Unblinking.

He pulled the covers back and stood. He didn't look around.

He took a step toward the balcony door. Took another. When he reached the door he opened it and stepped outside. Had he taken off his robe before climbing into bed? He wore it now. His bare feet cushioned by ratty green thongs he was sure he had discarded years ago, they carried him onto the balcony and into the fog billowing over the railing. He walked through it blind, farther than surely the balcony reached, but still walked knowing he wouldn't fall despite the rational thoughts that said he was about twenty feet above the ground and nothing under him. It rolled around him, swelled and arched over his head and then it began to clear. Light without a source illuminated the moor onto which he had stumbled. He didn't blink, and stepped ahead.

Tufts of land stretched above black waters that gently lapped at land's edge. Crabgrass and cattails blew in a light wind; nothing jutted from the water. The ground was soft, moist but not muddy—more like sand. He walked slowly. The fog hung like a wall in the distance, surrounding him on all sides, and never revealed anything new except sporadic islands and still, black water.

In the distance he heard something splash, and picked up on something further away, writhing in the water. Unaware his own foot had slipped, he didn't look down until he felt the water around his ankle and found he couldn't lift his knee to take another step. Something had grabbed hold.

Drops of water crept up his leg, like fingers of a drowning victim reaching for help. He imagined an arm, the water like mercury sliding up, extending toward him, burning and now another arm, trying to pull upward, grabbing for his leg. His other foot slipped and Alec found he couldn't take hold. His caught foot began to give to the water, and he fell to his butt. His free leg bent and braced, he dug his hands into the sand and pulled. The fingers and arms were relentless, and he was slipping.

Panic set in; he pushed harder against the pull of the water and harder it seemed to reach and more he slid across the sand and down the slope. Now his robe was caught, and more fingers began tugging and groping. There was no escape. Nothing could get from the water, once it took hold, and he was meant to drown in this strange swamp before Karl ever arrived. The kids and Lisa would have nothing to save them, then.

His lips curled and his fists drove into the sand, burying in up to the wrists, and when it seemed they stopped he pushed them further, and knew the only way the water would take him then would be to rip his goddamn arms off because he wasn't going to go like this, and he kicked and pulled and strained and his mind was empty of fear and he was determined.

It caught him off guard, therefore, when it let go, and he rolled back and nearly splashed into the waters on the other side.

He rose to his feet and dusted the sand off as best he could. It was fine, though, and he chuckled to himself when he thought of how he was going to explain this to Lisa, and he realized it wasn't funny; his slight laugh was of fear. Soft grains sparkled against the dark fabric. The hair on his legs caught the granules but the skin didn't itch or burn, except where the water had dampened his foot, and there it scorched his flesh into a scarlet rash. One thong had been lost in the struggle, and as his bare foot touched the sand steam plumed and sounding far off, a howl escaped into the fog. He kicked the other thong into the water, realizing he had heard such a noise before, and with that he knew where he was.

The howl had been too much like the scream of a spirit dying, and this was where the dead and the children were brought when the shadowfolk came. He stepped to water's edge, crouched, looked out across the water. Sinewy features of long-dead faces, lost to the struggle of the water, now rested in their burial shroud. But where were the children? Absently the fingers of his right hand dug into the sand, swirled it and tunneled through it as all he saw in the water were ghosts. When it came to him he backed away, not paying attention to where he was going, and nearly fell in the water again. Even then he couldn't tear his eyes away from the sandy dunes jutting above the waterline at his feet, stretching for as far as the fog would allow. Alec saw how many had been lost. There the girl from Georgia, crying out to him, reaching

155

up for him. Other children now just granules sprouting weeds, reached their sandy hands toward him.

Alec screamed.

He sat up in bed, sweating. His sheets smelled of urine, and when that fully registered, he blushed. The reading light at his desk, and the touch lamp at the head of his bed offered enough light to show him his robe flung over the back of a chair; he threw the sheets back expecting to find his own legs caked in sand, the mattress sandy, his one foot that had slipped burning from that water. The sheets were soaked but only from him, and the embarrassment rose again. He stood, stripped the bed and wadded it all up. He began to carry it downstairs when he stopped cold from an afterthought, and added to the pile his robe.

The house left dark, his steps slow and easy, he made his way to the laundry room and started the washer. He stripped off his wet boxers and added them to the machine, as well as his pile, closed the lid and just as silently, walked back upstairs. He put on a fresh pair, still smelling the urine, and it was while he was debating showering that he heard the scream. It caught him, and without thought he raced down the stairs toward his crying son.

Lisa started awake to Billy's shrill and thuds in the hall. She began to rise, her mind still asleep, and heard the children's door tossed open. She took a step, fears acceptable only at night overwhelmed her and then she heard, as she passed through the library, Alec's calming voice. She stopped and listened. In muffled tones his voice carried through the house, reassuring his son that he was here and all was okay. It was just a bad dream, he told Billy. She watched for him to emerge from the room, and while she waited felt the night around her. Summer heat's undeniable taste wafted through the room, caressed her nose and throat and caused her to sway. Somewhere distant and without location brought her faintly to the aroma of lilacs, and the serenade of midnight critters massaged her temples. Her eyes began to close; she could smell fresh-cut grass now. She swayed in place. Vaguely she could see them all, through the shadows, watching her from all points of the library, silent, staring, as the night hypnotized her. But she wasn't scared. The shadowfolk weren't here.

The door opened a little and pulled to, and Alec entered. Immediately the smell of lilac and fresh-cut grass overwhelmed her, and with eyes barely able to see she smiled at him as he told her Billy was asleep again.

"Thank you," she said, trying hard to focus on him, nodding as he told her he had to go shower. "You can use mine," she offered and held out her hand to lead him to the master bedroom. He thanked her, followed as she led the way, and when the water began running she collapsed under the covers and lay her head against her pillow. Lisa began to drift and realized there was no difference between this feeling and inebriation, and just as her eyes closed the shower turned off.

Alec emerged and thanked her again. She reached out her hand and told him to come. He stepped near. She fought drowsiness to sit up, caressed the back of his hand with her fingers and her ears perked a little. She heard the washer in the other room, finishing the spin cycle and beginning to wind down.

"I am glad you're home."

"I know it's still going to take a lot of work," he answered, "for us, I mean."

She examined his body, let go his hand and slowly traced her fingertips up his torso. She swallowed and blinked, felt his chest and brought her hand back down to his flat, defined stomach. *Let him quit working out*, she decided then, *let him get soft*.

"Bedtime," she muttered, and he nodded, touched her hand briefly and walked toward the library door. She called out to him, catching his attention and as he turned, she folded down the covers on the other side of the bed. She hoped he could see her smile in the darkness. He must have. He slid under the covers and she felt him tremble. He moved toward her. With hesitation their arms embraced, and only through her prodding did they intertwine their legs. She rested her head on his chest, squeezed him and heard him offer a sigh before squeezing her to him. They fell asleep quickly like that, and as she awoke the next morning, she felt him still holding her. She smiled, began to roll and lifted her arms to wrap around him also, when she had turned.

She stopped, the smile dropping from her face. She examined her hands, brought the left one closer, traced her right index finger over the back of her left hand. She hadn't realized something was still missing. She had forgotten about it, as a matter of fact. But now, illuminated in the fresh morning light, she remembered what it was, and saw how ugly her hands looked now.

Glancing over at him she saw he was still sound asleep. Her eyes blinked slowly as her lips spread, and she felt it all uncontrolled. He was breathing evenly, his countenance peaceful, indicating rest, peaceful dreams. Dark circles had formed under his eyes, so prominent she had wondered how long it had been since he slept. Probably over a year now, she assumed. But as the light brightened his face, she saw the remnants of the circles lifting away. Slowly, so as not to disturb him, she rolled away, giving her back to him.

She slid the top drawer of the bedside table open; his arm draped over her didn't budge. She stretched, reached toward the back of the drawer and removed a leather box. From it she removed a ring that, at one time, had been two. It was gold, and over one of the bands was a 1/3-carat diamond. He had given that to her first. The second gold ring, a band, she had received when they promised before God and their families that they would love each other for the rest of their lives. She examined the ring with contentment, then slid it onto her left ring finger. When it was secure on her hand again she faced him, and watched him till he opened his eyes.

FIVE

The Last Time They Met

Hospitals have always left Alec Bradshaw feeling discomposed, and this rehab center is no different; the cold penetrates the goose bumps and the lenitive atmosphere makes him feel more like a patient than a visitor. He looks up to the camera in the corner, examines the tag pinned to his shirt that reassures him he is only a temporary guest.

He sees the door open and two men lead in a third. The third is smaller than the others, wirier with hair as red as... he thinks "eyes," then pushes the thought away. The man has a dark countenance that makes Alec cringe.

The redhead man sits down as his ushers leave. He examines Alec with an ugly smile. "Do you remember when it all began?" the redhead man asks. Alec nods. He asks how everyone is doing. Alec tells him he and Lisa have since graduated, and married. They are expecting their first child. Alec's brother and Lisa's old roommate are living together now, with another year to go before they graduate.

"Do you remember when it all began?" the redhead man asks again.

"Yes. It began when I came back into your lives."

Karl waited for Alec on a barstool in a bar with its own microbrewery and fifty beers on tap. They were on Dickson Street, and Alec knew as he walked into the smoky room, that of all the people he

159

missed, Karl was the last one he wanted to see. But it was Karl who called and pleaded. Alec knew if ever there was a chance to return to the group, this would be it. So he came.

"I'm going to California," Karl said to start. He lit a cigarette, and waited for Alec to respond. Alec smiled, felt the rush of triumph, and then Karl continued. "Reality shows are becoming very big now, and I'm going to pitch one involving us."

"What's the show?"

"We spend a night or two at haunted houses, document things with a video camera. We'll research the place and you'll write the script for it, telling the history, the legend, whatever. We'll all take turns with the camera, exploring different things, trying to catch something on film. Lisa can conduct physics experiments around the haunted areas to try and find a scientific explanation for what's going on, and Cory and Justine will be responsible for finding the next place we're to go."

"And where are we going to get the money for this?"

Karl smiled. "I have enough for our pilot episode." Alec was about to ask when Karl thought they could start, as Karl's smile broadened. " And I've got the first place already picked out."

Karl's grin made him nervous, and Alec ordered his first beer in months. He sipped at it twice; decided he had outgrown the taste, and pushed it away. He watched Karl, staring at nothing, smoking a cigarette, smiling, and something in his eyes.

"Have you been to see Lisa yet?"

Alec hung his head. "Not for three months. When do you want to do this?"

"In another month or so, just before school starts. You need to see her."

Alec shook his head, surprised himself when he spoke softly. "I don't think she wants to see me."

"You're all she's thought about." He stamped out his cigarette, blew smoke and looked at Alec. "I'm not coming back to school. When you guys start I'm going to be hitching to California."

"Sounds dangerous." Not really, but Alec had found that he could care less where Karl went or when he left.

"So is what we're going to do," Karl said, his grin returned. He dropped it, softened his eyes and looked at Alec. "Go see her."

Alec hesitated at her front door, thought about trying for an excuse, found it impossible when the door swung open. Lisa stood there, leaning against the frame. She wore red shorts and a white t-shirt, her umber hair down about her shoulders, framing her viridescent eyes; every curve of her body accentuated by a paragon line. He approached. She looked up at him and, wrapping her arms about his neck, she pressed herself close.

They sat in the living room of her duplex catching up; Alec told them about roofing and working out, when they asked about his tan and body. Lisa told him about swimming at the lake and working with little kids at the pool.

"We've missed you."

He took her hand between both of his and laid it in his lap. "I'm sorry."

She laid her other hand atop his, sighed, gave him her eyes. He wrapped his arms around her waist and laid his head on her shoulder. He could smell her shampoo. He could feel the softness of her skin. She didn't wear a lot of makeup; she was the prettiest girl he had ever seen. He wanted to hold her all night, just like this or spooning in her bed—he didn't care which. They all sat in silence for some time, until Cory suggested they watch a movie. The one they picked they watched in silence, some scary film where the ghosts were violent, a somber film whose chills resonated beyond the credits to their beds as they tried to sleep later, so dark that it couldn't have a happy ending, just an ending.

He pulled Lisa close, kissed her forehead. She asked what's up. He said nothing, shut his eyes, felt her rub his stomach. He thought of the movie, of Karl's idea also.

"What scares you?"

She didn't answer right away. "When you were gone. I didn't know how you were doing or what was going on. I was worried."

"I'm okay," he reassured her.

"That movie was pretty scary," she admitted. He smiled, gave a chuckle and felt her slap his chest. "Glad that amuses you."

"No. I was just thinking of that. And what we're going to do."

"My brother told me once when I was little that mirrors are actually cages that hold things back," she said, her voice caught between a whisper and a normal tone. "He said you get more than seven years bad luck." Her tone shifted. "He said you let things out, when you break a mirror."

Alec, despite himself, started laughing. "You're scared of mirrors?"

She slapped at him again, rolled onto his chest and bit down. He howled, held her close and hoisted her up and rolled with her till he was over her, staring down to her face. "Pretty stupid, what we think as kids," she said.

"Pretty stupid," he admitted. He kissed her. He stopped before anything else could happen, rolling off her and huffing. "I left because I was afraid. I was afraid you wanted Karl, and I was pissed that a friend would come go behind me and try for someone who is obviously so important to me."

"He tried," she answered. "I didn't." They fell asleep together, holding each other tight.

A week before the fall semester was to start, the five of them drove to South Arkansas. They drove through an exiguous town —the birthplace of Alec and Cory's grandfather—which had been prosperous around the turn of the century thanks to an oil boom. They passed Daly Pond, where their grandfather had seined bait in the slews, swam in the waters, hunted and camped. They drove down a dirt road that spurred off a homely collection of houses and dead-ended with a cul-de-sac behind Daly Pond.

Through the trees, they could just make out a raised mound running the length of the road. On it were remnants of railroad tracks, Alec explained, pointing out the cross planks and metal ties. The Union/Pacific hadn't run this spur in years, but once it carried the timber in the area up to the Missouri Pacific Line and from there, to all points around the country.

"This is where the legend of the headless engineer started," Karl interrupted. Alec shook his head. He had heard the story many times, and Karl was already screwing it up.

"He wasn't an engineer," Alec corrected, regaining all their attention. He stared out the window to the tracks, imagining the tale, picturing it so well he spoke with reverence. "The tracks are elevated, and every time it rained this guy went to check the tracks to make sure the ground beneath hadn't washed out, which if it had could cause a train to derail. If he found a section washed out he'd warn any oncoming train by swinging his lantern.

"Only one night it came up a bad storm, and the Union Pacific was late to pick up the next load. He tried to warn the engineer that a section of track had washed out, but it was too late. He slipped in the mud, his neck landing on the rail, and unaware of what was happening, the engineer rolled the train on, decapitating the man.

"His head was never found. It was probably drug down the line by the train, maybe snatched up by wolves. But every night, two miles down this spur, you can see his lantern swinging as he searches for his head."

"Swamp gas," Cory scoffed from behind the wheel.

"Is that where we're going?" Justine asked, her voice shaky.

Karl said no and pointed to an isolated house at the end of the road.

The house was a two-story wood with a tin roof, an edifice standing amid the trees, illuminated by the afternoon sun. Weeds engulfed the drive and bound the lower story, blending the home into the landscape; a weed itself withered now, like driftwood washed up among creeping moss.

Karl walked up the porch steps, tried the screen door—which only sagged off its hinges when pulled—tried the front door and found the lock had been busted out. He opened it and led them into the hall. There was no furniture in the house, but the walls and ceilings were covered in mirrors. Lisa jumped at her own reflection, offered a tense smile to Alec. He contemplated reassuring her that nothing would pop out of the mirrors tonight; instead he patted her shoulder and led her into the living room.

Dust carpeted the floorboards. Some light made it through the windows, but Karl still brought a lantern in and lit it. From outside limbs rustled against the windowpane and inside everyone felt the touch of a zephyr prickling their flesh.

"You know this one too?" Karl asked. Alec looked around, nodded. He held Lisa tight to him and took it all in.

"Our grandfather was a young man, about to enter the military for World War Two, and this house had been standing for fifty years. A black family was leasing it then—Andlin, I think. One day while he was still waiting for his orders, he went to the General Store. Mr. Andlin pulled up with two of his children and his wife. Our granddad said his wife was like wood.

"Mr. Andlin led his children inside and bought them an ice cream cone. They sat out on the steps with our granddad while he walked back in. He walked out a minute later, said something to his wife, then sat down between the kids, an arm around each. The sheriff pulled up fifteen minutes later and arrested him."

"Why?" Lisa asked.

"He had buried his oldest daughter alive about a week earlier, and came to town to confess. He said she had been running around with some white boy and he was going to learn her from that. The police searched the house where he said she was buried…"

Karl pointed to their feet, a grin on his face that made them uncomfortable. "She was buried under here, four feet down."

"Only they couldn't find her," Alec added. "Just some message she had scratched with her fingernails while fighting for breath."

Karl knelt, feeling along the boards, pulled up a square section to show them the underside. The dirt below moved with night crawlers and meal worms, the wood rotten with termites. Lisa gasped and Justine clung to Cory. Karl smiled. The nails had to have broken off long before the one-word message was complete, but Alec could see her, fighting for breath, switching fingers as one was worn to a nub. Each letter was stained dark; time had worn them away nearly, but they could still make it out.

SHADOWFOLK

Alec read it aloud, his lips trembling.

"You did that," Lisa said, staring at Karl.

He shook his head. "I just did my research. I don't think she was running with a white boy. Her dad said that, and probably accused her of it, but I think she was sacrificed." He paused, grinning with bared teeth at each of them before turning to Alec. "Finish the legend. It gets better."

Alec swallowed hard. "The girl roams the house at night, seeking retribution against her father but taking it out on anyone in the house. An old lady who moved in here during the 1950s figured that out."

"This isn't fun anymore," Justine said. Cory squeezed her close.

"The old lady put all the mirrors in. She had heard the legend and felt sorry for the girl. The old lady, it seems, had a ton of money and never married. No man was worthy, so she stayed alone, and came to stay with the girl who was now alone too. The old lady died here, the girl her only companion."

Alec frowned, looked to each of them before finishing. "She was lonely. You can see her reflection in the mirrors still, watching you. At least that's what the story says."

Lisa looked around, trying not to look too close at the mirrors. "I don't think I want to stay here," she said.

Karl stood and began walking toward the door. "Tough. We're here tonight. That's the deal."

Cory grabbed his arm. "What if we all change our minds?"

Karl laughed. "You people. I tell you we're going to stay at haunted houses and you're all for it, until you get there and get scared by a couple of ghost stories." He stormed away. All eyes on him, so also the somber face, faded enough to be camouflaged by the reflections of the tangible, smoky and drab with only memories of the physical, the old woman watched her new guests, and felt the shadows move.

Caught in his own memories of that night, the redhead man stops talking. His face hangs, numb from remembrance. When he looks up again he looks at Alec for the longest time, a sad look, pitiful, as though he dare not say it aloud, but he is silently pleading for help. His bloodshot eyes and furrowed brow remind Alec of a mongrel dog, untrusting of humans because every master has beaten it, homeless now because nobody cares to take it in. Alec looks away, stares at the floor.

"I saw the girl that night, Alec."

Alec nods, says he saw her too. The redhead man says she's the one that led him from the house, took him to Daly Pond. The ghosts, he says, weren't the worst thing they faced. Alec asks him where he was going when he left. The redhead man doesn't answer right away, and when he does he is frank.

"I was going to wake the shadowfolk. I wanted Lisa back. I don't think you should have her, and I was going to get the shadowfolk to help me."

Alec glares at the man, clenches his fists, but before he can react the redhead man continues. "She was so beautiful in the moonlight. It's like they led me outside, brushed me out as the house sighed its stagnant air. If I could have seen her, though, seen what they had done to her, if I could have seen them swim around me, through me, I wouldn't have done it. I would have run and left you there. All of you. We woke them up, Alec. I woke them up when I followed her to Daly Pond. And now they aren't going to stop."

Even after two years, there is fear in his eyes. Alec looks around the room, expecting to see what the redhead man sees, hoping he doesn't. Alec asks him what happened at Daly Pond two years ago. The redhead man won't answer. He begins to shake, and for just a second Alec sees something dark creep below the skin of this patient. Then the redhead man laughs.

"They caught me with meth, this last time, at the half-way house. The first time I came to the rehab center it was for some pot I tried to hide in my pillow. It was just pot, and they want to send me to rehab when I take anything, and send me to lock down when I don't. The drugs are the only thing that can keep them at bay. I'm damned either way."

Alec asks him what the shadowfolk are, to which Karl shakes his head. "You saw the tape, didn't you?"

Alec had watched it after they returned home, something he wanted to forget.

"Ghosts are memories of the past, Alec. The shadowfolk devour those memories. Ghosts haunt places; the shadowfolk haunt people. And when they're strong enough, *when they can't be stopped…" his voice trails off and his lip quivers. "Old stories are hidden, nearly lost in the Deep South, of families living in shanties, gray wooden homes with tin roofs and you could lay in bed at night and look up and see the stars. Families of eleven living in one or two room homes on a couple of acres, raising their food, cooling milk and other spoilable items in the river or a spring, churning butter, slaughtering what they raised, everyone with chores and no television or electricity, and as late as this century, the only transportation still on horses. Walking in at night to see that shadow, sometimes the shape of a man, sometimes a fog, always blacker than night, watching their little children, asleep in their cribs, with eyes as red as the blood in your veins."*

He takes a moment to reflect, or—Alec surmises—to contemplate his own sanity, before he asks Alec what happened that night, at the house, while he was taking a swim.

Alec dropped the video camera to his side then looked at his brother. Cory sat on the windowsill smoking a cigarette, staring at his own reflection in the hall mirror. His brow was furrowed, his lips pursed, and Alec noticed a shake in his brother's shoulders.

"We haven't found a fucking thing," Cory said. His voice was always shaky, his tone clipped.

"No one said we would." He set the camera down facing the stairs and squatted by the window.

"So what the hell happened?"

Alec shrugged. He was growing tired of Cory's incessant need to curse. For kicks he threw one back at his brother. "What the hell do you mean?"

"With Lisa?"

Alec's fingers discovered that grout had built to sludge between the floorboards, and the camera was auto focusing on something just down the hall. "I slowed down."

Cory nodded; even his sighs had an edge. He looked at Alec in confusion. "That doesn't make a damn bit of sense."

Alec shook his head. "We drive fifty miles an hour to gas up our cars, so we can speed to some place we really don't have to be, or we don't have to be so quickly. We're always doing something, or going somewhere, and we treat everything in life like that. We set time limits on ourselves, like time is the ultimate constant."

The camera sputtered.

"Time isn't a constant. Gravity affects time. Time is integral to space—inseparable really—and is largely based on perception. A day could fly by for you and the same day could seem like the longest of my life. I got sick of it."

"So you slowed down?"

The camera tried to zoom. Alec glanced over and saw nothing in the camera's light.

"I've known her for eight months now. I slow down and that seems like a lot longer than you may perceive it. People used to not be in such a hurry, and for them eight months would be more than enough time to decide if you love someone. I slow down, and I realize it's the same for me."

Cory nodded, flicked his cigarette out the window. Alec stood, stretched, looked at the camera again. The light over it reached a few feet, but whatever it was focusing on wasn't within the light cone. Cory seemed to take notice of the sound and stood by his brother, watching the dark end of the passage where the stairs led down.

He pushed Alec's shoulder. "Go get the damn thing. Hold the light up. Maybe we'll see what it sees."

Alec shook his head. "You go get it."

The camera whizzed. Cory pushed him harder. "Get the damn camera."

Neither of them moved. Footsteps echoed from the landing, ascending the stairs. Slow, even steps, heavy, like something was taking undue effort in walking toward them. He thought of the girl, buried alive, struggling more to leave an obscure message at the cost of her fingers than to dig herself out. The footsteps reached the top of the stairs, five feet from the cone of light. There was a pause. Another step was taken. *Maybe she won't step into the light,* Alec thought. Another step, and with it a dusty print of a barefoot sole appeared on the floor. Everything fell silent.

Lisa ran her hand along the banister, feeling the dust cake the grooves in her fingers. Formulas and theories filled her head—ideas already considered but not fully tested like the effects of radiation and electrical currents on the natural environment. She didn't have the necessary equipment to perform such tests, but she could theorize. She set her bag on the floor, not thinking about the inscription. Justine squatted next to her, tracing her fingers along the floorboards, pressing her fingertips against the wood, then her nail.

"Her fingers must have bled like crazy."

Lisa thought about what happens when something smothers from lack of oxygen, and said that would have been the least of the girl's worries. Lisa heard her sigh, felt Justine's eyes on her.

"What's wrong?"

"Do you believe?"

Lisa tried not to think of such things. Things like believing in ghosts, or something her older brother had told her once about mirrors, were too much of a distraction, and only made her cringe. So Lisa shuffled through her bag, preparing to do the few experiments she had the resources to perform.

"You can explain three of the four forces that govern the universe with quantum theory, but gravity seems so far to deny it. Well, there's an argument that gravity can be governed by quantum mechanics, if we think of its attractive nature in terms of strings—it's called string theory."

"God," Justine yawned.

"In order for string theory to work, though, the universe—the entire universe including our galaxy and our planet—has to be made up of either ten or twenty-six dimensions."

Justine shook her head. "What do you mean dimensions? Like 'dimensions'?"

"Like three space and one time dimension. Like height, depth, length and time, it's what we live in."

"You're saying there's more dimensions than that?"

Lisa shrugged. "Could be. Has to be if string theory is to work."

"So we don't live in a four dimensional world?"

"We do. That's all we need to survive in this world. But there are other dimensions. Maybe here they're just folded up into themselves too small for us to notice."

Justine frowned. "How the hell can you even call that an answer to my question?"

Lisa smiled. "Those dimensions are too small for us, maybe, but maybe not for what we call ghosts. Maybe that's how they get here."

Justine nodded, then frowned again. "They use those other dimensions to get to us. Where do they come from?"

Lisa shook her head and huffed. Quietly—as the color left her face—she asked Justine to hold up the lantern. She exhaled again and shook. Her breath crystallized in the darkness. Then she heard her brother's voice, an echo only, warning her about cracked mirrors. "Things can get out," he had told her, "when mirrors break."

She stood, her eyes focusing to the hall. Beads of glass refracted the lantern light; there was a chip in the bottom of the mirror next to the door. Lisa held up a finger. There was no breeze. From her bag she pulled out a small mercury-filled thermometer. The mercury was falling at a steady rate. She took a step and Justine caught her arm. When she looked back Justine let go, held a finger to her lips and pointed. There was a cracking sound that intensified as it neared, a familiar sound, like ice settling in a glass of water. Her eyes widened.

Lisa snatched the lantern out of Justine's hand and ran to the wall. Kneeling, she found the chip in the mirror and saw the fissure heading toward a door jam. She backed away, held the light out and searched for the fracture line. It inched forward. She moved the light over; her eyes fixed on the crack as it neared the edge.

The crack slowed down, and the mirror behind them quivered. She stepped back; fingers shuffled her hair. She rubbed the back of her neck as the mirror behind her began to spur, and then she stared ahead. She trembled. The mirrors were cracking; they were going to break soon and then…she tried to push the thought away. It kept coming. She looked around the room, around the darkness, found Justine's hand and began to pray. *Don't let them break*, she whispered in her head. *Please God don't let them break…*

Alec and Cory passed the girls on the way down; Lisa looked shaken. He asked her if everything was all right, and she nodded, averting her eyes. He looked to Justine, who pressed her lips together. He exchanged a glance with Cory then walked on down with his brother. Cory took the video camera and was now filming the cracks in the mirrors. Most had a single fault, but some had spider-webbed. These were hot to the touch and vibrated slightly, a hum distinct at contact with the fingertips. Tiny cracks had begun jutting out from the single lines, and Alec knew it would be a matter of time before they frayed. His answer to fear and stress was to block it out, so he knelt by the radio, turned it on low to some rap station out of Little Rock, filled mostly with static. He flicked the dial and found a rock station just a little clearer.

A burst of static interrupted the music, and Alec decided Karl must be off getting stoned. From behind he heard Cory say his name, excited about something. Alec uttered a what and Cory said something about the mirrors still cracking. Alec turned his mind away and tinkered with the volume.

Nothing had appeared in the camera. He had reviewed the tape through the viewfinder with the hopes of seeing something. Its audio recorded only the sound of the house settling and their voices. The rest must have been their imagination. His first impulse to record over it with the downstairs footage was finally quelled; they could review the whole thing later through the VCR.

We're jumping at shadows, he thought, as he heard the static build again, masking the singer. He looked ahead to the front door. Behind him, Cory said the glass was too hot to touch. On the radio the tone changed underneath the static. Cory said the mirrors were shimmering—the word he used. From the corner of his eye, Alec saw light dance as the mirrors waved. Then he heard voices.

The voices sounded like interference playing over the music. Only that seemed wrong. He turned up the volume…louder whispers and louder static. He turned it up again, fidgeting with the tuner, until the voice broke through.

"GET OUT OF THE HOUSE!" it said, repeatedly, until there was a noise like a swarm of wasps and the voice screamed. Alec jumped back, staring at the radio; no sound could compare to the pain, the fear in that shriek. The stridence reverberated through the house, and the house responded. With a similar piercing all the mirrors exploded.

They bounded up the stairs, and finding Lisa and Justine on the landing between the first and second floors, they cradled them, shielded them from the flying glass. Alec was the first to see them step from the shattered mirrors.

Many of them, shaped like men, sanguine eyes watching the four of them, encircled them. Justine screamed and they watched a young black girl mount the stairs. Her fingers were worn to bloody stumps. Her white dress was wrinkled and muddy, her skin once the color of chocolate now ashen. Her head lowered, tangled hair fell over her face. Lisa prayed she wouldn't raise her eyes. She did.

The solid white filled with blood, as she smiled, until her eyes were red, swirling, and the pigment of her skin crawled. A flash tore their gaze away, even caused the girl to look. The old woman stood above them on the second floor, shaking her head, unaware that the shadowfolk were closing around her. She frowned, reached out to the girl and then screamed again. The shadowfolk had begun to devour her.

She writhed at first, tried to fight, but they swarmed, consuming her. Her scream echoed, and for the second time that night Alec thought his very soul was going to shatter. But he didn't cover his own ears to block the pain. He covered Lisa's.

When they were done they scattered, and the scream died like a fading echo. The four of them left alone, frozen on the landing, unsure if they should move or not. Lisa was the first after it all subsided. She looked up at Alec; he could just see the tears as her eyes searched his for solace. He whispered it was okay now, but he didn't let her go. She rested her head on his chest, sighed. He rubbed her back and kissed the top of her head.

Alec says he had watched the tape a few nights later. Lisa was in the shower. Cory was studying at the library and Justine was working late. "I didn't really expect to see anything."

Karl asks what he saw, and Alec says he burned the tape. He took the radio to the landfill and tossed it, and since then they have talked about it once. Karl asks again who was coming up the stairs, and there is an insidious glint in his eye. Alec imagines them fluttering around Karl, wisps of shadow with sanguine eyes.

"She wanted you to help her, before the shadowfolk made her scream."

He had almost missed it; the camera shot at thirty frames per second and on two of the frames there had been a glitch. He had paused the tape, stared, climbed to the screen. A young girl stared ahead, shimmering, smiling.

"She was looking through the camera, right at me."

Alec stands to leave and stops. He can't look at Karl, instead his back is turned and his head is hung.

"What happens when the shadowfolk are strong enough?" he asks, and it is a while before Karl answers him. Alec wonders if Karl even heard him. He's ready to ask again when Karl sighs deeply and answers.

"Be wary of your coming son, Alec. You and Lisa both. Don't let him sleep alone at night."

Alec steps for the door, his face hot, his vision blurred. Karl asks his question. It's not one Alec is ready to answer truthfully, but he does, after Karl asks it a second time.

"Why, after two years, did you come to see me?"

"Because I received a videotape in the mail." He doesn't feel the need to be more specific. No, he tells Karl, he hasn't watched it yet. He doesn't have to. He knows what he'll see.

He reaches for the door, knocks. The guard opens it. As Alec is leaving Karl calls out, "We'll be seeing you again," and Alec senses the grin on Karl's lips. Something else he'll try to not think about, and he turns in his visitor's pass and walks out the door.

It was the first part of August when Alec awoke from this dream. He rose quickly, sweating, the bed empty. The children had briefly joined them in their bed for about a week, then went back to sleeping in their own beds, giving him and Lisa solitude. Their lovemaking lasted the entire night, ending with them cuddling and whispering the few hours left till dawn. The tension was there, buried by the lovemaking and sharing the bed, and it was fading slowly. It would be gone, he realized, if he didn't know the inevitable was about to happen. *She'll hate me again*, he thought, looking at the empty bed, her impression on the mattress still evident. Far off he heard a door shut and could just make out footsteps on the floor. He looked at the clock, it read 9:00. The room was hot with sunlight—the drapes had been pulled back and the mini-blinds raised—and he realized something else, as his head began to clear. Something had shaken him, screamed at him, just as the dream was ending. Someone wanted him awake.

Karl's here, he thought, and alertness replaced the fatigue. His bright eyes sharpened their focus on things in the room, and his mind began to list what had to be done today. Beneath all that, a saddened heart reminded him again that Lisa would hate him, when he has to leave again.

The bedroom door opened and Lisa entered, smiling, plopping on the bed next to him. She ran her hand over his chest and kissed his cheek, her eyes meeting his. He squeezed her close and kissed her forehead, as she said "Morning, sleepyhead," and he asked if she got the kids off all right. She said she did and they kissed again. Then there was silence, the only sign that tension was still there. He asked what she had planned for today and she said nothing, she wanted to spend it with him. He said he had a few errands to run in town and then he'd come back and take her to lunch and spend the whole afternoon with her.

"You don't want me to come with you?" she asked.

He thought about it, wondered how he could explain where he had to go and what he had to do. He finally settled on the truth. Said he was coming down with a case of "Adult-itis" and wanted to check on boring grown-up stuff like insurance policies and money in the bank and financial matters and all that stuff. He added a lie and said he wanted to check with the community college for a possible teaching position.

She stroked his chest. "You have to do this today?"

He didn't want to. He wanted to hold her all day, naked under the sheets until it was time to pick up their kids.

"You know how I am. I get something in my mind and I have to do it right then."

She laughed a little, rolled atop him and kissed his lips. "Well you better get going so you can get back."

He smiled at her, stared longingly into her eyes. They had come a long way. He wanted to finish the journey with her. But he didn't allow himself to contemplate that yet. He dressed, kissed her and promised he'd be right back, only using his eyes to reassure her, to quell her unspoken fear that he could be abandoning her again. She didn't want to let him go, and he didn't want to leave her arms, but he did and drove to town. The first thoughts came as he sat in a corner office of the bank.

Staring at the burgundy trim, listening as the pretentious woman in a pant suit outlined all his accounts, the money in his father's trust now accessible to him and his family, he thought about the dream. There would be more than enough money for them to run, and was that—he asked himself—the reason he had the dream now. So they could run. Or could they run? The shadowfolk weren't bound to structure. They were tied to people. Could they ever escape, then? Or would they just keep running? There was enough money to get them off, and perhaps get them settled someplace new, but not enough to keep running. Bits and pieces of the dream fluttered in his mind, forcing shivers from him, and it was as though he had repressed it. The fact that he could forget such a night, that it could seem so alien now frightened him, and he wondered if he were truly ready.

He sat in a cubicle at the insurance office, listening to more good news as he concentrated on the part of the dream concerning his last meeting with Karl. The dream took a new turn, then, as it still haunted him, but seemed more familiar, and his meeting five years ago with Karl seemed like yesterday. The insurance agent—another pretentious woman but more plump—told him his grandfather had left enough money to pay off the policy on the house and land, which his father had seen to years ago. Lisa had used some of the money he had sent—she must have because she didn't make enough on her own—to make sure their life insurance was paid up. It had in fact been kept up for two years, which meant if something were to happen now, the policy would be paid out in full. His voice quivered as he said that was good.

His lawyer asked if he were sick; Alec looked down and saw he was trembling, felt the sweat beading on his arms and forehead. He looked at the old man who looked like a ghost, said he may be coming down with something, and asked him to continue. The wills were in order. Lisa and the kids were the beneficiaries. Alec surveyed all this and realized they may have enough to keep running. But it wasn't until on his way home that it all hit him. He pulled to the side of the road, grabbed his hair and fought the tears, and dry-heaved.

He had been driving Lisa's car for the errands—hers had more gas—and as he pushed the button to raise the garage door, he prided himself on making it home safe, his mind as preoccupied as it had been. He could have wrecked.

He edged the car into the basement, oblivious to the quick swarm of darkness and someone sneaking in behind the back bumper, just in the car's blind spot.

He rushed up the steps after closing the garage door, not looking back, more intent on finding Lisa than worried about how someone could get in; he grabbed her, kissed her, held her tight. They cuddled until they got the phone call at the school; the children were sick.

He watched the children, too worn to move, barely eat, finally go to bed only to toss and turn and wheeze and whimper. They had skipped their baths. He stood by Lisa at the door, the closet light on—Alec wondered if it were enough—his arm around his wife, watching the kids drift off. The shadowfolk were in the house.

He could feel them, felt a tremor with the deceased members of his family. He squeezed Lisa's shoulder and led her away, back to their room—a notion that used to be enough to comfort him—laid her on the bed. She yawned. He touched her shoulder, allowed his hand to drift down to her thigh. Outside the humidity had built to thunderheads, lightning flashed around them. It was a brief storm. It would last long enough to dampen everything, and leave the morning just muggy enough to be called sticky. *There may not even be rain*, he thought, *just lightning*. He realized he was doing it again. His mind always turned away first, and then he always ran.

He pulled his wife close, mouthed the words "I'm sorry," though she couldn't see. He prayed in time that she could forgive him. She was drifting slowly; he could tell she was worried about the kids and that was delaying sleep. His mind turned away again, told him what to say to Lisa if he ever had the courage.

"I know why the kids are sick," he would tell her, he should tell her. "The shadowfolk are here. Karl is with them. Don't worry. I know how to stop them, but it's going to cost something. It's unavoidable, but I've got to do it this way. It will cost us this house, and I will be gone."

He perfected his little speech, adding "I love you" here and there, and telling her how important she has always been to him and that he's doing this for her and the children.

He said none of that.

"Hacimos ruidos por la noche."

She looked up at him, offered a little smile, squeezed him. Then she nestled herself against him, her head back in the crook of his shoulder and neck. He waited till she was asleep, recalling the times they stayed up all night, wanting another chance to see the sunrise with her. He began to pull away; she had latched on, and he had to reach slowly around his back and unlock her hands. Then he began to roll. She started to roll with him. She stirred, and afraid she was going to wake he stopped. He waited. When Alec was sure he began to roll again, slowly lifting Lisa's arm draped over him while not putting too much pressure on the arm under him. *Just let her sleep now*, he thought. Let her and the kids rest, and I'll wake them when its time, if anything should happen before morning. He knew something would, he knew the shadowfolk were here and Karl was somewhere in the house. He knew something would happen before morning, because he was about to force it; he was going to find Karl.

SIX

A Visitor to the Home

Alec gave one last look down at his wife sleeping. She curled up, and for a moment as a hand stroked the mattress, he was afraid she'd feel no body and wake up. If she woke now, if she woke as he walked out of their bedroom, it would ruin everything. Lisa and the kids had to stay asleep.

He walked slowly across the room, dressed in shorts and sandals and a t-shirt, opened the door to the laundry room and closed it behind him. Not a light on, clouds hid the light of the moon. As well as Alec knew the house, he still had to move slowly and feel his way. He heard the latch take, loud in his head, and he caught his breath, listened. She didn't wake. There was no movement, no ticking grandfather clock, no mockingbird. His fingers traced the wood trim, moved to the paneling and felt the groove of a sharp corner. They traced along the next wall and found more trim. He dropped them a little on the surface, continued sliding them right till he felt the round metal of a brass doorknob. He curled his fingers around it and tried to turn it. It wouldn't budge. He reached to the face, felt the ridged circle in the middle of the knob, turned it counter clock-wise. Trying the knob again, it now swung open. A draft blew up from the downstairs, and he met blackness. *Down there*, he thought to himself, nearly pointing.

His foot touched the first step with a creak, his left hand felt along the rough plaster to smooth plastic. He felt the light switch, flicked it, saw down to the bottom. A pool of light illuminated the concrete floor at the bottom of the stairs, but the blackness walled up at the edge. *Lots of spaces down there*, he thought, and took another step. He closed the door behind him, realized he had no power to lock it from this side, pushed the thought away. He'd do what he had to do down here and go back upstairs, wait with the door locked. He reached the bottom, flicked on the basement light, and his eyes fell directly to the partition separating the basement/garage and his father's old studio.

Against the wall sat an old electric heater. It had sat there for years, and as far as he knew hadn't been turned on since his grandfather had lived in this home. So attuned to that heater, to that answer, he missed the shadows as they moved. He missed the sanguine eyes, and the lanky figure stand ten feet behind him in the spur of the basement mostly hidden where there was a bathroom. The figure that was once a man smiled. In its hand was a small wooden bat.

Alec walked quickly to the heater, examined it: the wires were frayed and the case dusty. The elements were built with grime, and the partition just behind it was dry with bits of insulation protruding from its cracks. He knew beyond the outlet, the wiring would be just as rough. All he had to do was turn it on—he flicked the knob to three, the highest setting, and felt the heat warm his body and face—and jostle the wires, then wait till it warmed up; he moved it, stretching the wire without unplugging it.

He straightened. The faulty wiring would have no trouble releasing the energy, and the insulation would be good fuel. Shadows danced, eyes watched and just behind him the bat was raised. He said a short prayer for Lisa, for the kids, realized he'd have to make some coffee if he were going to stay up the rest of the night. Even if the shadowfolk didn't attack tonight, even if Karl wasn't here, the wiring could go at any time, and this house would go quickly. He had to stay alert, then; he had to stay awake.

The bat came down. Alec fell to his knees, stunned, unsure of what was happening.

The bat came down again at the base of his neck. His vision blurred and he was on his stomach.

The bat came down a third time, and he found he couldn't move.

Tears distorted everything he saw. His vision blurred at the sight of a tall, redheaded man walking slowly up the steps, turning out the light just as Alec's vision dimmed.

But he could hear. He heard Justine calling out, pleading not to be taken from her daughter, begging to no answer. And then she screamed, a sound Alec hadn't heard for seven years.

He tried to stand, tried to push up with his arms. He couldn't. He collapsed, his head slapping the concrete floor, he felt something splatter and could only assume it was his own blood. His world went black again, and as he left the scream faded, like a dying echo calling from across a still lake, where black waters allowed nothing to escape and only lapped at the sandy shores.

Somewhere beyond, he heard laughter.

SEVEN
The Morning

Lisa awoke to an empty bed. She sat up a little, stroked the mattress where her husband had lay, looked around. Her husband; the sound of it in her own head made her smile. To make love to him again was—she searched; the only word she could come up with was … inspirational. Yes, to make love to Alec was inspirational. To have him hold her was inspirational, or sit and talk to her. She sat up in bed, smiled, her arms bracing her up with elbows locked. Her head down, her face and vision shrouded by hair; she tossed her head back and her hair whipped. Her chin up, she closed her eyes, felt the sunlight enter the window and warm her. It was going to be a hot one, and by this afternoon the humidity would be up. *It may storm*, she thought, trying to wake up.

She thought the word again, "inspirational," and giggled. *God, did they smoke something last night?* She chuckled. To be fair she tried to remember the last guy to make her feel the way she had with Alec since first meeting him. There were several men who had tried to play her emotions. They were gone. So what was it that had kept her from discharging Alec? There weren't children then. They weren't married, and now…

Now he was back after running for six months. The fact that the legal separation had been mutual affected her mood at intervals. Sometimes it made her remorseful of the past. Other times it made her angry. Now she found the question prodding, the one question that always brought out anger. Alec's assumptions led to his actions, brought out complacency that was fed by fear and caused him to run.

Why the hell didn't he fight back? Why did he give up so easily?

She was in the shower, washing her body, trying to get the stream of water to wash away her feelings. The hardest part she thought would be the confrontation. That came a month ago, when she thought he was leaving again. A confrontation would seal the emotions, keep her from loving him one minute and hating him the next. But while the confrontation had tamed her feelings, they were still there. That was just the first step. Hashing everything out made it clear where each stood, and it made something more clear to her now. Nothing will ever be the same again. Nothing will ever be perfect between them. Soap-laden water swirled around the drain, vanished, and she realized the kids would be up soon. She got out, toweled off, and found herself back at the starting point. Why go through all of this with Alec? Deep down she knew, and it made her giddy again, until Billy screamed.

Her robe was on, her hair was wet, but she was dressed enough. She darted from the bathroom and through the library, into the kids' room. Billy was twisted in his covers, his head cocked back and looking at the door. His eyes were bloodshot, a dewdrop of snot hung from one nostril. He sniffled and the drop hit his pillow. His cheeks were puffy, and when he spoke or breathed his lungs sounded full. She glanced over at Kimber, her sheets stained from sweat and urine, smelling. She coughed; her lungs like Billy's sounded full and wet. Lisa leaned on the doorframe and stared at them.

"I'm thirsty, Momma," Billy said, then doubled over and hacked.

"Do we have to go to school today?" Kimber asked.

Lisa shook her head. She told them she'd be right back, leaned and kissed her son and then kissed her niece. They stirred in bed, watched her with crusted eyes, didn't try to rise. She said she was going to put some clothes on, checked their hot foreheads and walked out. She missed the marble bust as she passed through the library, the blood welling up at the corners of the eyes.

She walked into her room and changed quickly into shorts and a t-shirt, slipping on her sandals. She looked around, noted Alec's absence but didn't allow herself the time to wonder where he was. She walked back into the library and turned, stepped into the bathroom and grabbed the thermometer from the medicine cabinet. She would give it till noon before calling the doctor. Outside there was a clap of thunder. She walked across the hall to the den, peered out the blinds and saw trees doubling over. She noticed Alec's car was still in the driveway. She sighed but not much relief came. She heard nothing upstairs and forced away any questions to his whereabouts. As she stepped back into the hall she walked toward the stairs, turned in place and finally called his name. There was no answer, and she missed the shadows, swirling from corner to corner, watching her.

Billy's temperature was 99.8 degrees; Kimber's was 100.1. Lisa watched them, doubling over, coughing, both soaked enough that they should be thirsty, they should be dehydrated. She lifted Kimber out of bed first, tried to set her on her feet. Kimber crumbled to the floor. Billy did a little better; he was able to pull himself from the bed and stand, but Lisa could see it was taking all his effort. With a quick motion only a mother could possess, Lisa stripped the sheets off the bed, smelled the urine and sweat and recoiled, wadded all of it up into a ball and tossed it to the corner. She knelt, helped Kimber to stand. The little girl only swayed, head cocked, her eyes barely open, watching Lisa without blinking as Lisa pulled off her panties and shirt, tossed them onto the pile. It was when she turned to the girl's dresser that she heard the explosion.

She stepped from the room, looked around. It had come from nearby; it had come from the library. The door had closed a little, so she pushed it open. She saw immediately what had happened, and she nearly screamed. Billy's voice kept her under control.

"What was that, Mommy?"

She had heard a scream with the explosion, she realized. It was brief, more a cry out, but it had been there, accompanying the sound of the marble bust shattering. The face of the bust had split in two, and jagged fragments in shards about the carpet. What really got her though, what came and nearly took all control away, was what she saw around the eyes. Tears reddened the eyes, painted the cheeks pink and were forming a maroon stain on the floor, saturated now enough that it was nearly a puddle. She pulled the door closed and looked at the kids. Both were pale, their eyes glazed and they swooned where they stood, as though the shadows were massaging them. She led them, directed them back into their room and made them stand while she pulled a pair of sweats and a t-shirt out of a dresser and slipped them on Kimber. She found Billy his own sweats and t-shirt in another drawer, dressed him, and then led both kids to the den. A part of her wanted to carry each, but she made them walk, made them exert the effort. As she picked up the remote for the television, she finally asked herself where Alec was.

She turned on the television to a cartoon where a little girl was teaching kids the lessons of order and throwing in a little Spanish, got them two glasses of water, and called the doctor. The appointment was made for two that afternoon. The lady answering the phone said if they got worse to bring them on in. Outside the clouds built and darkened. Lisa sat between them, cradling each one in her arms, watching the cartoon with them. She felt like crying, worried as she was; both were pallid with red-rimmed eyes and both were dehydrated. Billy took two sips of water and threw up on the floor, bile. Kimber managed to finish hers, but vomited soon after. Lisa cleaned both messes, grabbed two well-lined wastebaskets and put them within reach of the children.

Not a lot of rational thinking consumed her mind, concerning them. Most of it was feeling, a sadness in her heart to see the kids suffering as they were. Her rational thoughts were of Alec, praying wherever he was in this house he'd come find them. A horrible idea planted itself, and she grew angry for thinking it because it couldn't be true, and angry with him because what if it was. What if he left the car, just took off on foot, walking away?

The television blinked, the lights flickered and then they were left in darkness, heavier from the thunderheads outside. The foundation shook, and both children squeezed into her. Kimber asked what happened. Billy barely looked her direction.

"Power went out," she explained. She saw another flash of lightning out of the corner of her eye and held them tighter. She looked out the blinds and the rain seemed to be blowing in circles, trees whipping in the wind. Then it all stopped, and Lisa grew nervous.

The sky was green, the rain had slacked and the wind had stopped. She gave the children a reassuring pat and stood. Billy reached for her and she reassured him it was all right. She told them she wanted to check on something, said she'd be right back, and realized that if it was about to hit she'd have to drag two sick children barely able to stand down to the basement. She wondered if she had the strength, knew she'd find it. She opened the door and tried to muffle her scream with a gasp.

The mockingbird lay on the welcome mat. Its legs were turned up, its feathers were frayed, beak open. Its chest had swelled, as though it was in the middle of a deep breath when it just dropped. She slammed the door, missed the swirls of darkness stretching from the corners, noticed the cleaned mantle. Then she remembered the bust. The grandfather clock began ticking, stealing her attention. The bust had exploded, the hummels and mockingbird were gone, all signs of a previous life were being wiped clean. And the children ... there was something about the children. She backed away from the clock, staring, trying to convince herself that it was nonsense. She had to maintain control. From the den Billy called to her.

Fear crept upon her, impressed itself on all she was seeing as she tried to deny it. Karl was sick. Billy called out. Karl was locked away. Billy yelled, hoarse. There was nothing here. Her son groaned. The shadows whispered and she thought she heard a laugh, distant and hollow and devoid of joy, filled with hate. She shook it off and squeezed her eyes shut.

She felt like a child, standing in the entryway, shutting her eyes and clenching her fists until the scary part was over. She wanted to weep when she heard the song, a whisper that crawled into her ears, from a crackled old voice straining to be heard.

"You are my sunshine
My only sunshine
You make me happy
When skies are gray."

Trembling, her eyes blurred, her cheeks wet as she thought of the two kids in the other room—her kids. She began to sing along, her own voice strained.

"You'll never know dear, how much I love you, so please don't take my sunshine away."

It was her son's cough that brought her back around, and with a sigh that left her hollow inside, she wondered where her husband could be.

EIGHT
The Storm Worsens

If there was a tornado, it had missed them. The rain and wind resumed, came in torrents and left them in darkness. Howls and whistles called from around the eaves, the windows vibrated and the lightning gave them a bittersweet reprieve. The children napped.

She stood, paced a little, watched them. Their fingertips were red, their flushed cheeks collapsing. They were hot and dry to the touch, their flesh as powder. She watched their chests rise slowly, fall a little, their lips just parted. She swallowed hard and decided two o'clock wasn't coming soon enough. She glanced outside where it was not letting up, and thanked herself for parking in the basement, not having to drag the kids out in that.

"Shit!" and she looked at them. They were undisturbed by her burst. There was no way to get the garage door up. She watched them, made sure they weren't going to stir, turned and walked into their room. She gathered up the pile of urine stained sheets and clothes and carried them down the hall, through the kitchen and into the laundry room. The idea came to her that she could drench it in Shout, put it in the washer for when the power returns and get it out of their room so it could air out. She glanced over to the key rack and nearly cursed again.

Alec's keys were gone. She looked away, shaking her head, trying to deduce where he could have put them—they were normally hanging up—and then she looked back. Something was wrong, something was out of place. She studied it. The key rack still held her keys, and aside from a painting hanging crooked, there were the two doors at right angles to each other, the right leading down to the basement and the left to her bedroom. She frowned. Unable to place it at first, but slowly her concentrated brow furrowed. The knobs of each door held a lock in the handle that could either be set vertical or horizontal, depending on whether the door was to be locked or unlocked. Both locks were horizontal. Lisa swallowed hard. It had become ritual since the phone call from a concerned psychologist to make sure the lock to the basement door—as all doors granting access to the outside—was turned vertical.

Alec was down there; what concerned her was who was with him.

She reached for the door. If they were here, if they had found Alec, then he was dead. The realization hit her like ice, raced through her. She was sweating, her hand trembling. Her fingers graced the knob and stopped. Outside the lightning flashed and she heard another clap of thunder. Could she do it? Could she open the door and see Alec splayed in front of her, more than likely bloody, definitely broken? Cold. Lifeless.

From above she heard a creak.

She looked up, locked the door, unaware of what had happened to Alec, or that he had come to and, while still in pain, unable to stand, had pulled himself halfway up the staircase before collapsing again. She ran to the den, the house's dark ambience lost to her no longer. The shadows were more prominent, taking more effort in revealing to her that she and the kids were not alone.

Billy was awake, staring at her as she rounded the corner. He didn't move, and in the few minutes she had been gone he seemed to be worse. He called to her, his voice strained, a whisper buried under the noise of the storm. She sat between them again, an arm around each. Their fevers had broke, replaced by a chill as cold as the metal locket around Kimber's neck. The couch and their clothes were drenched, but their skin was dry as though no sweat had seeped from their pores. Lisa looked up, the ominous corners of the home out of reach of the daylight were all the more formidable. They were watching, waiting. She heard another creak overhead.

Billy squeezed her hand and began sleeping again. She stood, walked around the corner to the base of the stairs, looking up. She couldn't tell if the door was open or not, couldn't remember if it had been shut or open before. She grabbed the banister and took a step, another creak directed her gaze up. She caught her breath, stared, and did a very stupid thing. She called out for Alec just as another creak resounded. It seemed to stop short, and all she found was stillness. Shadow undulated along the wall, billowing up then down. She gripped the banister tighter, unable to tear her eyes from their focus. The door was going to open, she realized. She took another step, listened for footfalls and heard nothing. She took another step. Halfway up she heard another creak, closer. Her breathing deep, uncontrolled, she couldn't blink, and knew if she let go her hand would tremble. She took three more steps and was nearing the landing at the top. Two more risers at the top of the landing, to her right, would lead her to the door—shut, she noticed—and then to the creaks. There was another. It sounded just in the hall, just on the other side of the door. Another creak. He was going to reach the door before her. She glanced back—and then he'd have her.

The kitchen phone rang, and something happened that shouldn't have. The portable in the den rang. She looked down, listened for creaks and looked back to the door, afraid it would open. It didn't; she raced downstairs into the den and snatched the portable up. She dropped it, covered her own ears as a noise she had spent seven years trying to forget erupted, and the children awoke. The scream echoed through the house, and she forced herself to let go, listen to the maddening sound as she reached for the kids, startled with fear just hitting them. She covered their ears, stared ahead and rocked them until the sound subsided. What she heard was the faint voice, as familiar as the scream and just as distant, calling to her from over the portable.

Quivering she let go the kids, reached to the floor and picked up the phone. Her eyes wide, trembling, she put the phone to her ear.

"Hello, Lisa. It's been a while."

"Where are you?" she asked, but she knew.

"I brought some friends to play with Alec's family, Lisa. Now they want to play with your kids. You and I can play too, now that Alec is done."

Her face reddened and she threw the portable across the room. It smashed against the wall, shattered, and from above she heard a triumphant giggle filter down. When it died she heard the creaks, saw the room darken. She snatched up both children, carried them in her arms, not wanting to stop but forced to at the base of the stairs where the hall turned to lead into the kitchen. She was panting and her arms were hurting, and both Billy and Kimber were hanging, dragging their weight. She held on to them as she sat them down, then looked up. The panting stopped. The sweat froze to her brow and she couldn't move, couldn't look away.

The upstairs door opened. The walls moved in waves of shadows, crashing and spilling downward, toward her.

She hoisted them up with a grunt and forced herself to not look up. They rounded the corner. Dark swirls darted along the walls, whirled about them. She had Billy just under his arms. His feet drug on the linoleum and pulled her down. In her other arm, Kimber was twisted sideways and bent backward, tongue lolling, eyes closed. Lisa made it to the kitchen when the whistling began.

She had to set the children down in the laundry room again, catch her breath. She could hear him, taking his time on the risers, he was whistling something, and the shadows were drinking all the natural light in the house. Billy couldn't keep his eyes open. He was mumbling, barely conscious, cold to the touch and—not near as bad as Kimber—his skin was wrinkling and flaking. Kimber was unconscious, her cheeks and eyes sunken, powdery flesh that rubbed off on Lisa's shirt and skin. She opened the door to her bedroom quietly, carried both kids in and lay them on the bed. She raced to the door leading to the library, locked it, turned and jumped.

There was a knock on a door. She stepped toward the laundry room, heard it again just above Karl's whistles. Had he heard it too; the whistling stopped, the footsteps stopped. Even she stopped, except for her fingers, caressing the lock, then, ever so slowly, turning it. She gripped the knob, wondered how close was he. Just right around the corner, as the shadows suggested, or further away. She began to turn it, watching the silhouette on the wall elongate, a shuffled boot along linoleum whispering in her ear. Unmoved she looked to the left, to the door, her body still facing the kitchen. And then it all happened at once.

The door hit something—it groaned in response—and there was a noise like falling and the shadow sprung and then Lisa was following, toppling over and her cheek slapped the wooden stair, and then her arm and shoulder and then her face again and then her leg and hip and then her back and she felt it would never end; she had no time to cry out just fell and twisted and smacked her body over and over and she rolled over something fleshy that gave and then she was on her side.

Unable to move, barely able to breathe, her eyes winced and her flesh burned. She gripped for the cement floor, grain dug into her fingertips, under her nails, and the floor was cold. There beside her a hump, which obscured the base of the stairs from her blurred view. It barely moved, but it was breathing. The door swung open to a silhouette of a tall man whom she hadn't seen in five years. His grin prominent, his teeth and red hair illuminated through the darkness, he glanced over his shoulder, into her bedroom, and brought his smile back, before descending the stairs.

NINE
The Shadowrealm

Billy understood a lot of things—more than most would credit a five-year-old—especially now that death was staring at him with its blood-colored eyes. He understood the sky was blue because Dad said the sunlight made it blue when it passed through the air. He understood to lie was wrong and cursing was what stupid people did when they didn't know anything better to say. He knew about life, and life was precious, and he knew the shadows didn't care about that. They were here to take his life and take the life of Kimber.

They weren't scary at first. At first they were only black clouds moving around the room. Then he saw the eyes. Now they looked like men and the only thing he could really see were the eyes. Everything else was dark, and he prayed the power wouldn't come back on because he didn't want to see what they really looked like. And he could hear them.

They talked amongst themselves in whispers. Too weak to run, all he could do was look at them and he didn't even want to do that; he didn't want to hear what they had to say. He wanted his mom—he assumed it would be all right to call her mommy right now, although he did feel too old most of the time to do that—and he wanted his daddy. But the man was with them, right now; he understood that too. He was the one who brought the shadows.

He understood that no one could stop them. He heard the man screaming at his mommy and daddy and he couldn't hear them, though. He just knew that no one could stop them. So when he saw Uncle Cory standing aside, watching, getting mad, and when he heard Uncle Cory speaking to his head, Billy was a little surprised.

"Don't you worry, Billy," his uncle was said. "Your mommy and daddy are okay, and they'll be here soon. And I'm here. We won't let anything happen to you, Billy. But I need to show you a few things. Can you hear me okay?"

"Yes." Billy was a little surprised at how weak he sounded.

"They shouldn't hear me. You have to see these things, Billy. Will you watch them?"

Billy was fading. He tried to nod, but the shadows were close, and as Cory showed him the first thing Billy thought he couldn't watch. But it was so beautiful, and Billy smiled. Light, just a little, returned to his eyes, as he watched.

There was a long stretch of beach and water as far as the horizon, as blue as Daddy's eyes. A strip of a town was behind the beach, and behind that, trees and grass the color of his mother's eyes made the hill overlooking the town. There was no shadow; and the sunlight made everything bright and gold. Cory explained it was a little town far away, and after they left here they could go. But he had to fight, Cory told him, so he wouldn't end up here.

The hills shrank away and the town bled into the sea. The sky darkened and Billy knew that this was where the shadows lived. It was dark and misty, and if he knew the word for a marsh he would have called this one, with tufts of land jutting out of murky, black water. Billy gasped, and the shadowfolk pulled away, and he heard a couple of things. There was a loud pop and his mother screamed. Billy still saw the marsh, but he also saw Cory running, screaming, raising a fist as he jumped into them. And then Billy saw a ghost die.

In the marsh the scream was louder, the death-throes tossed the still waters as Cory sunk down. The water was black and hard and thick, and Cory couldn't pull away. He sank, screaming, his spirit pulling off him—he grabbed at one and pulled and the shadow writhed as it sank into the water, and then it was empty, and Billy was left alone.

He stood on a patch of land, looking around the mist, understanding that his uncle showed him this because it would help him to fight. Cory had wanted him to see it, because the action Cory had intended came through. Determination grew in Billy's heart and he frowned. He didn't know the word determination but he knew the feeling. It was what his dad called not giving up. He stepped to a side and peered over the edge to the countless faces of spirits trapped beneath the surface. He listened to the sounds hidden within the mist, growling noises and spitting noises and lots of crazy things that little kids shouldn't hear when they are alone. He took another step and heard a scream; the ground had come alive.

He jumped, froze, as children's faces raised out of the mud, calling to him, begging for release. He screamed and began to cry as hands of mud and sand reached up for him. And Billy understood. The children, devoured by the shadows, were also brought here, made into the earth upon which the shadows tread, so the shadows wouldn't fall into the water. Or made into the earth for something else to walk, and he heard it again. He shivered, took another step…he couldn't. He couldn't move, he looked down and saw his feet covered by the mud. He looked around and saw all the children trapped, reaching for him, calling to him from their place in the sand.

From the mist Billy saw the shadowfolk approaching, through the mist looking just as they had at his house. Through the mist he saw them as they closed in, heard them whisper, grew afraid as they neared until he sighed to a familiar voice and the mist broke where one stood.

Smiling, his grandpa faced him with bright eyes and outstretched hands; Billy nearly ran to him. He stopped though, even as the man beckoned, and watched the shadowfolk beckon too, still behind the mist, just behind the man.

"Come here, my child. Come with us. Me."

Billy stepped back, and quickly the mist rolled over what looked like his grandpa. Still it called, though its voice changed in the fog, "Come here, my good boy. My *catamite*."

The shadowfolk stepped beyond the screen and slowly more than just their eyes came into focus. He saw jaws and nails and realized they looked nothing like men at all. Billy screamed, pulled everything from his lungs he could.

TEN
In a Blaze, Death

Alec pulled himself to his knees, shook and felt his side fall away. He clutched at it and felt only wetness and something soft pushing its way down. His head went light and he coughed, but not blood. He looked up and his eyes stung. Smoke rolled toward him, black, burning his flesh and eyes. And he couldn't remember everything.

He remembered pulling himself up the stairs one riser at a time, because—his head went fuzzy—because he had awakened. He had awakened and he had been hit and it felt at the time like his neck had been broken. He rose to his feet near the top, pulled himself up the wall, only to fall again. Lisa was there.

He pressed his right fist into the hole in his side, listening to the scream upstairs. No ghost was dying this time. He twisted his face into a grimace, his lips into a snarl. It was the sound of his son dying. He stood, swayed, fell against the wall and looked up through the smoke. It raced ahead of him, and from behind he could hear the pop of wires burning and insulation being swept up and it wouldn't take long for the foundation walls and support beams to become embers, and then the house would fall. And upstairs, just beyond the black smoke, Billy was being murdered.

He started to crawl. He took a step, fell back, nearly fell onto his ass. But he couldn't let himself fall that much, so he caught himself, slid along the wall, and to his left something exploded. The studio enflamed, the gear engulfed, a monitor had exploded and in its light he saw something lying on the garage floor. Something Karl had dropped after Alec took the bullet. Karl had dropped it to chase Lisa, who heard the scream first. It was all coming back, now. Alec bent, snagged it off the cement floor then made it up two steps before falling. His legs gave and he lay on his back, staring up as the smoke rushed around him, burned him. He closed his eyes and heard his son scream again.

Lisa kicked and this time it connected. Whatever hold Karl was effectively pinning her with had slipped, and this time her throws found a source. He cried out, she saw an eye too close to her hand, bunched her fingertips and gouged it. He fell against the dresser. Lisa jumped into the middle of shadowfolk; she could just see them biting and clawing at the children, and the children, their screams muted, lay there. Withering, they didn't even fight back. They looked … she couldn't allow the word to pass her thoughts. With futility she reached for the shadowfolk, but there was nothing to take hold of. She looked at Billy again, at Kimber, and she didn't have the strength to fight when Karl pulled her back. She began to cry.

He slammed her into a dresser, loomed over her, staring her down with burning eyes, his face red with bulging veins. She coughed, and noticed something that had escaped him. The basement door was open, and smoke was billowing into the laundry room. His back was to the door, but surely he could smell it by now? He could, she realized, watching him. He just didn't care.

"Stupid little bitch," he said, balled up one fist and backhanded her to the floor. She spit a little blood, saw him overshadow her. "I'm trying to help you and you are too stupid to realize it." Smoke like tiny worms wriggled through the carpet fibers. Her palms began to burn; she lifted them and her spit puddles bubbled. Heat was coming through the floor. She doubled up and crumpled to the ground, her side lit up again with pain nearly worse than when she had fallen down the stairs. He pulled his foot away, crouched over her. "Stupid little bitch," he said again, as she closed her eyes from the pain and felt the spray from his lips and heard it sizzle as it touched the floor.

* * *

Something was coming out of the marsh, and it didn't matter much that Billy had found Kimber. He held her hand as she tugged at him, her eyes wide. She asked him what it was and he shook his head then tugged her hand to keep quiet. "Owe" she barked and then looked, because it was splashing and writhing in the water and Billy had seen the water and nothing could escape from it. He had seen Uncle Cory get drowned in the water and now something big was coming out of it. He was afraid, because as they ate at him he could feel them. And the shadowfolk were afraid also.

* * *

Alec touched linoleum, raked his hand back until it felt the door jam and his fingers caught. He pulled. His cheek touched the floor and it burned, but he didn't pull away. He only had one hand to pull—his right still jammed in his side—and he had little strength left after pulling himself up twenty steps with one arm, fingers already clinging to something. When he touched linoleum he had to drop it to grab the door jam and finish the pull, and now he curled it back into his left hand, drew his legs up and slid over the floor. The smoke was thick, but he could see more into the bedroom. Lisa was on her knees, the children were on the bed. Karl was crouching beside her and the shadowfolk engulfed his children. He pulled himself forward, watching until his vision blurred and then he had to shake his head until he could see again. If he fired now he might hit Lisa. He had to wait. He inched closer.

"I'm just trying to help you," Karl said, and he reached up and stroked her hair.

"Then call them off my children," she said, not surprised there was a hint of begging in her tone, caring even less. "You've already taken Alec. Don't take them."

"You just don't understand," and his voice began to rise again. "You just don't understand; I'm doing all this for you. We can have a new life."

"I don't want one with you," she said, and with that he rose. She felt his eyes on her. He stood straight and brought his foot back and then forward. It connected with the same side and she crumpled, crying out, doubling up and vomiting from the pain. She saw the foot go back and start to come forward, the toe right to her eyes. She looked over to the bed. Kimber's arm draped off the foot, her locket with her hair hung over the side. Lisa's eyes brightened at the glow of the locket as the foot connected with her jaw and a puff of smoke stung her eyes. Then she heard the gunshot.

The children had decided to run, and in the end they could not have done more. Running made them huff. Kimber asked Billy over and over what it was they were running from and he wouldn't tell her, he couldn't. He told her to run and don't stop and he could hear it getting closer but they couldn't stop and then he saw the hands reaching up from the marsh and heard children crying out to them and when Kimber asked what they were he told her to close her eyes and run and he'd hold on and lead her. But where were they running? From what, that splashing thing getting closer and closer? It didn't matter.

In the house on the bed the shadowfolk had withdrawn, and if they had countenances they would have seemed quizzical, because no child ever escaped them. That would be like a ghost escaping the swamp, and that just didn't happen.

Somewhere in the shadowrealm, whatever was chasing Billy and Kimber finally broke free of the water. There was a scream, but this time it was from the formless mouths of shadowfolk.

⁂

Alec found enough strength to stand, and it all came from seeing his wife writhe in pain and his children dying. He emerged from the smoke, gun in his left hand, his right fist in his left side, and stepped into the bedroom. Karl turned; he had lost the use of his leg due to Alec's bullet, and hobbled in place to face the laundry room door. Surprise was on his face that became doubt as he saw Alec step into the room. He shook his head and pointed. He said, "No" over and over so vehemently his red hair whipped around. Alec wasn't worried or scared. He had crippled the leg Karl liked to kick with. That was a nice start.

"You're dead," Karl said.

Alec raised the gun and shook his head. Then he pulled the trigger. Nothing happened.

⁂

From below there was a pop in the foundation, and Lisa made it to her feet. She watched Karl scream and pull clumps of red hair from his scalp. He took a step toward Alec, but as he took the next, she grabbed the dresser and stuck out her foot. He fell onto his face, and Lisa unveiled all the strength she had left. She pulled at the dresser—red oak like the bed and bureau to match—and it tilted. She pulled and the items decorating its top slid to the floor and then it rocked back. So she huffed, pulled and as Karl pulled himself off the floor at arms length the dresser slapped him back into the carpet. From behind Alec the fire spit up from the basement. Lisa had no time to deal with that, now. She pulled the locket off Kimber's neck—and the color was returning to their cheeks, moisture to their cracking skin—and began to swing it wildly. She could feel them in it, around it. She could feel Cory and Justine, and knew that it was more than just her swinging the locket—it was Kimber's parents striking out at them. She screamed out with rage; the locket connected.

Wisp forms recoiled from the blows, trailing smoky contrails as they retreated. She continued swinging, and the veil over the children began to recede. She kept swinging until it was gone and she fell into the kids, wrapping her arms around them. There was no breath from their lips, no open eye to relate consciousness. She began to cry. Alec stepped off the door and moved toward her, hobbling, holding his side. He dropped the gun to the floor and pulled his fist away, gushing blood all over the floor. He hoisted his son into his arms, and behind him the paint on the bedroom wall started to blister. She pulled Kimber into her arms and stood. Neither moved. The floor split with a groan and Karl and the dresser were gone into the flames. Surrounding them were the shadowfolk, closing in.

Billy and Kimber ran through the swamp hand in hand, and the little fingers of devoured children reached from their bed. Billy heard the splashing and it was closer, and to be honest Billy was tired. He didn't have the energy to run anymore. He was winded and tired and all but dragging Kimber. It would be so easy to stop and lay in the swampy tress and let himself sink in. They slowed, and from behind he heard the water break loose its hold, and something grabbed them.

The shadowfolk screamed, scattered as Cory walked out of the flames. He grabbed one, pulled it back screaming and kicking. The shadowfolk turned on him, encircling Cory and tearing at him and would have drug him back into their waters if the room hadn't brightened. Five orbs of light appeared, swirling out from the shadows, turning the dark penumbras of men into clouds as they tore away. The lights swirled around the shadows, knocked them into the flames. The screams of the shadowfolk were a more horrible sound of death than Alec could imagine, but he watched with a smile, until the shadowfolk had no where to run and, surrounded, they fell away into the flames.

Cory appeared among the family again, smiling. The house was creaking loudly and Alec felt the floor bow. He looked down at his son, so still, his flesh mending and yet there was no breath that he could discern, among the smoke and heat. He looked up to his brother, around to his family passed, and knew. Alec knew that if his son was lost, if the shadowfolk had gotten him, then there would be no need to for him to leave this house.

Cory reached up and opened the door to the library. The sound of glass shattering overwhelmed the fire, and the smoke began to race away. He stepped aside and the family moved. Lisa took the first step. Something exploded in the kitchen, and they all felt it. Lisa swayed. Holding the lighter of the two still pained her. She cringed, nearly doubled, nearly dropped Kimber but didn't. She stood and moved on.

"Take care of her," Cory said, looking at both of them.

Alec took his first step, felt his side burn and looked around. For him Cory had only one word. It inspired Alec to take another step, hoist his son higher and take another and another until he passed through the glass and into the front yard. Magenta light from the western horizon painted the low sky and stretched across the wet land. Still thick and black, the clouds had plugged the rain for now, but lightning still flashed sporadically and the thunder rumbled. Heavy drops fell in spurts, not steady enough to be considered a sprinkle, but Alec knew it would resume. They were under a break; to the southwest and to the north a sheet of gray connected cloud to ground. He walked from the house carrying his son, not looking back. He fell on Billy, shielding him, not watching as the house imploded and burned. In the distance he heard sirens. They wouldn't make it in time. He reached across the grass and felt Lisa's hand, squeezed it, and all he thought about was that single word.

"Live," Cory said.

EPILOGUE

Phillipe had gotten to know the family well in the two years he had spent in their presence; he'd be sorry to see them go, despite the strange things he overheard. He fixed the wench—it had been a little tight—and checked the mainsheet, just as he had promised the man. The cabin looked in order, and staring at the ocean-worthy ship now brought sadness to his dark, leathery face, wrinkled and aged.

Phillipe hobbled off the boat and started down the dock, taking one look back at the boat they had named, The Family Homestead. *Such a strange name*, he thought at the time they had dubbed it. After seeing what their intentions were, he understood a little better. They had decorated the cabin strangely as well, since Phillipe last saw it. They had been getting ready for a week, and the man called him last night to say he wanted to meet and give Phillipe the last check and buy him a drink, if Phillipe didn't mind. Phillipe promised to check out the boat this morning, and found it in good working order. But the books they lined their shelves with, all teaching books and literature and science and several books about speaking Spanish and French and Italian and those little ceramic figurines that wouldn't last long when they got caught in their first swell. But what really concerned him were the children.

The bar across the street had sand in the front, its roof ordained with palm leaves; it was a cliché bar for central Florida, a real tourist trap. But this was where the man asked to meet him, so Phillipe agreed.

He sat down at a table, ordered a beer, waited, thinking about the kids. The boy was seven, the girl was four and very sweet. She was always up her uncle's butt, and Phillipe laughed at that. He had really been paid to teach the two kids to sail. She understood so much, and both kids were very smart, but the boy was quiet. What few strange things Phillipe had overheard between the mother and father were never discussed in front of the children.

His beer came and he sipped it, still waiting. He wondered how the publishing was coming along, and never imagined that to make a book could take such a long time. The man had written two in the span of the first year, and through an extreme amount of luck sold both. *They should be out anytime*, Phillipe thought as the man came walking up.

He was young, thirty at the most, and the St. Pete sun had tanned him well and bleached his hair, set off his blue eyes. *They are a beautiful family*, Phillipe thought, and could vaguely remember when he was that young. So long ago, and memories fade so fast, which is why his wife scolded him the way she did about going back out on the ocean when the man first approached him for the job. Then, of course, she saw the check.

The man limped to the door, he was lean and muscular—not like those guys on TV who wear bikini briefs and flex, Phillipe thought— and very handsome, but the limp worried him. It had grown less noticeable over the two years the family had lived here, but even today it was still evident. When no one was watching the man had a sad look about him. Now he looked at Phillipe and smiled, and took his seat across the table.

Phillipe asked the man if he was almost ready, and he said they were. She was saying goodbye to her parents who were just now coming around to the idea.

"They wanted to blame me at first," he told Phillipe, a smirk on his lips. "Lisa chimed in and said it was her idea, and then Billy reminded us all that he was the one who first thought of it."

"You got some smart kids, Mr. Bradshaw."

He nodded, and Phillipe watched his eyes glaze for a moment, the smile hang there. Then he reached into the leather satchel he had brought in over shoulder and pulled out two books. He explained them as he handed them to Phillipe.

"Your copies. The first is about my family, kind of a literary fiction that would be reclassified if they knew how strongly it was based on my life."

Phillipe smiled, read the back cover. It was hard bound and had its own dust jacket, which told of a young man learning about life as he was born into a family, collected memories and watched the family pass on. Everything he'd learn, the man confided, he'd pass on to his own family.

Phillipe turned to the front, wondered about the title. He wondered if the man really knew the legend that shared the same name as his book, its origins in the Deep South, ominous tales of children being taken and people haunted and ghosts swallowed.

He looked at the second book and realized yes, the man probably knew.

"*On the Road with the Ghost Hunter*," Phillipe read aloud. He smiled and looked up at the man.

"It's nonfiction."

"I'm proud of you," Phillipe said, and was surprised at how soft his voice sounded as he uttered those words. He had come to feel like a father; he and Edith never had kids of their own, never knew the joy of grandkids, and they were the closest he and Edith had. He didn't want them to go.

"Between the book advance and projected sales—I hope they're right because we're going to need the money—I think we'll be all right. I found a real estate developer near St. Tropez, France, who has some places to show us once we get there."

"You leaving at a good time, Mr. Bradshaw." They were missing the hurricane season by five months. Phillipe's eyes squinted and he lowered his chin, bit his lower lip. "Why you limp? You never told me that one."

Alec sighed, dropped his eyes and took a sip of beer, then raised them again.

"Two years ago we had an intruder in my family home. It was the house my grandfather built. I was shot in the scuffle, and during all of it an electrical fire ensued and burned the place down." He told Phillipe of the insurance money he got, how they barely got out of the place in time, the intruder burned in the fire. He didn't go into much more detail than that. "They paid my medical bills and cut us a nice check for the fire which we've been living on while staying with her mom and step-dad. Hell, that check is why I could afford to buy that boat out there."

Phillipe knew he wasn't telling everything, but he didn't press. He took another look at the two books in front of him and raised his beer mug. Alec clinked them together.

"To the past," Phillipe said.

"To the ghosts," Alec added somberly.

As Phillipe watched them drift away, he recalled the afternoon he and Alec had gone to buy the boat. It was sunny and still cool out, but Alec was wearing shorts. He still had a cane, at that point. They must have looked like a sight, Phillipe chuckled; an old black man and a young man in Bermuda shorts and a straw hat and a cane walking onto the boat dealership. The dealer must have felt sorry for them or something, that's why he was trying to get Alec to follow him to a collection of used boats. But Alec had been adamantly against that.

"No. Nothing used, nothing with a past. No ghosts."

The sun was behind Phillipe, and he felt more confident than anyone he had sailed with or taught to sail, that Alec could get that thing safely across the Atlantic. From where he stood he saw Lisa on the deck, shorts and sunglasses and tan and firm, smiling and chasing after the four-year-old girl who didn't want to wear her life jacket. Alec knelt over the wench, looking back to make sure Billy was okay at the helm. Phillipe smiled, and a gold cast was set upon the water which Alec and his family followed. He had taught Alec all he knew of sailing, how to tighten and loosen the main sheet with a turn of the wench, what the boom's position was for—if all else failed, Alec had an inboard motor that could give the ship power and plenty of gas to steer them—and how to navigate both from the equipment and charts and maps and from the stars. Alec had showed the kids the telescopes mounted on the sides, telling Phillipe he wanted to show them the Milky Way, when they were in the middle of ocean. He wanted to show them the craters of the moon and the moons of Jupiter and Phillipe was fairly confident they could see all, in the middle of the Atlantic.

As they disappeared over the eastern horizon, Phillipe turned and waved at Lisa's parents. He noticed the others afterward, realized Lisa's parents were oblivious to their company, and was frightened.

An elderly couple stood, bracing themselves on the railing. He could see through them to her parents.

Beside them stood a middle-aged couple. Dressed conservatively, the appeared to be upstanding, proud, upper class. They were transparent.

Next and final stood a scraggily young couple, the young man with greased hair and wore a t-shirt and tattered jeans, his wife a petite thing dressed simply. Like the others, their appearance did not obstruct the view he had of her parents. They all watched the boat sail into the horizon, and then they vanished into the evening sun.

Printed in the United States
28010LVS00002B/328-336